Where Witches Lie

Tempie W. Wade

Where Witches Lie

By Tempie W. Wade

Printed in the United States of America.

First Edition Print - ISBN: 978-1-7363975-7-2

Digital Edition - ISBN: 978-1-7363975-6-5

For more information, please visit,

www.TempieWade.com

Where Witches Lie

by Tempie W. Wade

A Novel

1570

East Anglia

"We've lost two ewes and one ram in less than a week," Thurston Saunders complained, angrily slapping his hat down on the small table and closing the door behind him. He cringed, and his ire quickly faded, however, when he noticed his daughter, Sadie, peacefully napping in the cradle by the window. He tiptoed over and smiled. Reaching down, he lightly stroked her cheek with his calloused thumb, careful not to wake her.

"Still no idea what's killing them?" his wife, Muriel, asked, heavy with child, bent over the long wooden table kneading bread dough, the smell of the fresh rosemary she had just added wafting on the air. Straightening up, she pressed her hands to the small of her back and stretched.

Their baby was due anytime now, and she was more than ready for this little one to make her arrival into the world.

"Nay!" Thurston replied in a softer voice as he removed his woolen coat and hung it on a nail protruding from the wall. "There is not one single mark upon any of them, not ours or the neighbors. It's as if their hearts just stopped beating and they fell over dead where they stood. That, along with the Stone's wheat crops dying and the Roger's fruit trees not bearing," he shook his head while exhaling sharply, "well, it is just too much of a coincidence. I am more and more inclined to believe there may be some truth to this talk of a witch being responsible."

"Witches! You and your silly superstitions!" scoffed Muriel, wiping her hands on the front of her apron before easing down into a nearby chair. "Are you sure you haven't been nipping the ale at the tavern along with the other husbands a little more than usual this week?"

"Why would I go there to drink when I have perfectly good ale here? Besides, you are a great deal prettier and more pleasant to be around than those toothless tavern wenches," he teased before resting his hands on her shoulders from behind and leaning down to kiss her cheek. "I tell you, wife," his tone becoming more serious, "I *am* beginning to wonder."

"Well, 'tis a full moon tonight." She paused to chew on her bottom lip, attempting to conceal her amusement. "Perhaps you should go run a circle of salt around the sheep in the pasture. Just to be on the safe side, you might want to take off all your clothing, as well. I do hear tell those witches perform their evil dark rituals bare as the day they were born while dancing under a full moon. You wouldn't want to risk getting any part of it wrong."

"Maybe I will," he retorted good-naturedly, coming to stand in front of her. He cupped her face and kissed her again, this time on the lips with a great deal more sincerity. Drawing back a bit, he dramatically screwed up his face and asked, "Did you by chance save a foot from one of those rabbits I brought home a few days ago for supper? Maybe I should tie it on my belt for good measure."

Muriel reached over and took an apple from the bowl on the table. Taking a bite, she grinned and brushed the juice from her chin with the back of her hand. "You believe an animal's foot is all that is needed to save you from a witch?"

"I thought you didn't believe in witches," he countered mockingly, with a chuckle, light-heartedly changing the subject. Dropping to his knees, he caressed her belly and placed a kiss on top. "How's my son today?"

"Your *daughter* is being stubborn by not coming out to properly greet her mother and father." Muriel ruffled his hair with her hand.

"Must take after her mother!" he whispered in her ear, standing and pressing his lips to her forehead on his way to wash his face and hands.

Muriel watched him go, silently thanking the gods once more for sending this wonderful man into her life. Seeing him upset bothered her more than anything else in the world, and she would do anything to set his mind at ease. Waiting until she was sure he was in the other room, she ambled out of the chair over to the hearth and gathered a handful of herbs from a jar she kept on a nearby shelf. Tossing them into the fire, she spoke a few words. The flame shot up, turning a bright shade of blue as it emitted a distinct, colored smoke from the chimney. It was a signal to let the others know they needed to meet that very night.

Sometime after midnight, Muriel carefully eased off the bed, doing her best to not disturb Thurston. Stopping to peek in on Sadie, who was fast asleep in the small crib in the corner, she stooped down and planted a sweet kiss upon her forehead. She may not have physically given birth to that little girl, but she couldn't love her anymore if she had. Glancing back, she saw Thurston sprawled out, peacefully snoring loud enough to wake the dead, and knew he would be out for the rest of the night thanks to the valerian she had slipped into his stew at supper. That, along with the little satchel of fresh lavender beneath his pillow, would ensure he would never know she was gone.

Quickly dressing and slipping on her dark cloak, she bent down and kissed her husband's cheek before lighting a lantern and heading outside. The rest of the women were already at the cleared spot of ground in the middle of the grove of trees when she arrived.

"How are you feeling?" asked Evita Rogers, smoothing back her silvery hair as she came over to greet her. Evita was the oldest of the ladies in the group, the town's midwife, and Muriel's best friend since the day they met.

"I am weary and ready for this little girl to arrive," she replied. "I long to see my toes once more."

"It won't be much longer," assured Evita with a broad smile. "In fact, it might be sooner than you think."

"Well, let's get this other business over with so I can return home and get off my feet." Muriel turned to the other twelve ladies, of all ages and backgrounds. "I have called you together to address our not-so-little problem. We all know our husbands and fathers suspect a random witch is responsible for the bad luck with the crops and the dying of the livestock, but we know the truth—it is the angry spirit of our deceased former coven sister, Millicent Davies. Even in death, she is still one of us and it is up to us to deal with our own. Join your powers with mine, sisters, so we may have peaceful days in our village once more."

These women needed no further instruction for they were well versed and learned in their craft. Quietly, in harmony, they came together and formed a circle, shoulder to shoulder with single, white burning candles in one hand and a protection rune in the other. In the center of the group, one moved forward and placed a wooden box with ancient symbols carved into the top she had brought with her. Once it was in place, Muriel nodded and began to murmur a slow chant. Each joined, one by one, until they spoke in unison. With that, the wind furiously gusted out of nowhere, sending tree limbs crashing to the ground and threatening to extinguish their bond. However, the group held firm, strengthening their circle with their fortitude and holding their ground.

"She's here," announced Muriel with a wary glance towards the sky. "You know what we must do, sisters."

The members of the coven shifted their chant to a different spell, demanding Millicent present herself for judgment before a jury of her peers.

"By the power of all who have gone before, we command you come forth and answer for your actions!"

The reluctantly summoned spirit announced her arrival with an incensed, high-pitched wail. Against her will, she was drawn into the middle of their ring, cursing her sisters for their betrayal while trying with all her might to break the circle that held her in place.

When the coven's chorus refused to relinquish its hold, the enraged specter found herself being forcefully dragged down and into the box with a power she could not defend herself against. Her incessant struggle did not cease until she was safely secured with the lid slammed shut. Muriel quickly moved to seal the container with the wax from her candle, the others following her lead until every member had contributed to the conclusion.

"Now what should we do with it?" Alice Rogers asked, blowing out her flame.

"We will bury it on sacred ground, so no one will have to deal with Millicent ever again," replied Muriel, eyeing the small crypt in her hand. A brief flash of sadness crossed her face as she felt the vibration from the box, no doubt the witch's desperate attempt to escape. Resigning herself to the fact this had indeed been the only way, she sighed heavily and tucked it under her arm. After taking two steps, the pregnant woman bent over and groaned, a strong contraction abruptly overtaking her.

"I will bury it," corrected Janey Brown who immediately took it from her arms. "Right now, we need to get you home and in bed, so Evita can see your little girl safely into your arms. I think we all deserve to welcome a little goodness into this world after the darkness of this night."

"That sounds like an excellent idea," replied Muriel.

Evita slipped an arm around her waist and grinned. "You see, I told you it would be sooner than you thought."

"You forgot to mention it would be THIS night! By the gods, woman, a little warning would have been greatly appreciated."

"You are a powerful witch in your own right," teased Evita. "I shouldn't have had to tell you! You should have already known."

1

CHAPTER ONE

Brilliant flashes of gold and amber foliage adorned the tops of the trees, announcing the much-anticipated arrival of the season. The simmering aroma of pumpkin spice filled the crisp fall air, intermingling delightfully with the sweet fragrance of vanilla-and-cinnamon-sugar toasted pecans and cotton candy.

Cassie and her college roommate, Bethany, munched on their peanut-crusted-caramel apples as they strolled arm-in-arm among the many vendors, enjoying the town's annual Halloween festival.

The two stopped short when a solemn-faced little girl dressed in a long, dark dress appeared seemingly out of nowhere, blocking their path. Pausing to gather herself, the child straightened her pointed black hat covered in small silver stars before planting her feet in a wide stance. Producing a long, wooden wand from the holster on her belt, she proceeded to spin it in circles spectacularly in the direction of the two women. The pair looked to each other, thoroughly amused.

"Oh no! What have you done to me, witch?" Cassie dramatically clutched her chest and fell against her friend, delighted to play along.

"I have cursed you and turned you into a toad!" the youngster replied with conviction.

Cassie stumbled and pretended to fall, landing on one knee so she landed face-to-face with the child. "Ribbit, ribbit!" she whispered in her ear.

The little girl's stern facade instantly dissolved, sending her into a bout of giggles before running off to find her mother.

"Don't go!" called out Bethany, waving her half-eaten apple on a stick. "Cassie has a cheating ex-boyfriend we will give you twenty bucks to turn into a frog!"

Rolling her eyes, Cassie tossed what was left of her apple into a nearby trash can. "If she can pull that off, I will happily make it forty!"

Cassie and Scott had been dating for two months. Three nights ago, she had caught him in the act with a freshman cheerleader in his apartment. The bastard hadn't even bothered trying to explain himself, much less apologize, chalking it all up to 'the college experience'.

"I have a better idea!" Bethany took her by the arm, pulling her to one side. "If we are lucky, maybe one of these vendors will have a spell that will make his dick shrivel up and fall off."

"It wouldn't have far to go," muttered Cassie. The pair leaned into each other and burst into laughter.

"Look on the bright side. You are a free agent now and you can do whatever—and whomever—you like." Bethany smirked flirtatiously and nodded to a group of guys getting beer from one of the food trucks. "What about one of them? That blond is pretty cute and just look at his shoe size. You know what they say about shoe sizes being a good indicator of the length of something else!"

With keen interest, they stopped to size him up, their eyes immediately dropping to his feet. Their optimism faded, however, and took a hard turn for the worse when he proceeded to chug his drink—and promptly spew it all back up, along with his lunch. His friends cheered, egging him on by buying another round.

Grimacing, Cassie spun her friend around, steering her in another direction. "I don't know. I think I'm done dating men whose biggest goals in life involve beer kegs, frat parties, and banging cheerleaders. Besides, I think it is past time to face the fact that I only attract losers."

"Yeah, you might have a point," agreed Bethany, grasping her hand and pointing towards the section of tents set up for fortune-tellers, mystics, and tarot card readers. "You really *don't* have the best track record." She tightened her grip on Cassie. "Say, isn't that your archaeology professor over there looking like a Greek god having walked straight down from his throne atop Mount Olympus?"

Cassie stole a quick, nonchalant glance. "Yeah, that's him."

Dr. Thomas Armstrong had become the hot topic of conversation at the university. The word on the street was the administration had begged him to come to Stanford from his home in London to teach a few semesters. Being tall, muscular, and only about ten years older than his students meant his classes had become the most in-demand on campus. Add the fact he was single and sporting a sexy British accent also meant they were jam-packed with women, most of them not even getting credit for the class, it being so far out of their curriculum.

"Damn! I haven't seen him this close up before. Indiana Jones doesn't have anything on him! Have you considered asking for extra credit—or offering it?"

"NO!" Cassie pulled her away. "He is my teacher and that wouldn't be ethical."

"And morals are overrated! We are in college, and we are supposed to be learning from our mistakes," Bethany whispered back. "We should at least go say 'hi'."

"Even if I were interested, which I'm not, I am sure he doesn't even know who I am. There is no way he can keep up with all the students in his classes. The man has hundreds of them, and they are all women."

"Miss Summers!" they heard someone call out.

Turning, Bethany's face split into a wide grin when she saw the topic of their conversation was waving and hurrying over to them.

"Well, would you look at that? I guess he knows your name after all."

The professor, dressed smartly in jeans and a brown sweater, pushed through the crowd until he was finally able to make his way over.

"Dr. Armstrong!"

"Please, call me Thomas. Dr. Armstrong sounds like a family dentist with three ex-wives and a mean backswing. Besides, I am not that much older than you."

The on-point observation made Cassie laugh.

"You must be Cassie's professor," interjected Bethany, inconspicuously pulling her t-shirt down to expose a bit of cleavage. "I'm her roommate, Bethany Giles."

Dipping his head in acknowledgment and suppressing a smirk, he said, "It is nice to meet you, Miss Giles." Turning, he addressed Cassie who was uncomfortably rubbing an imaginary spot on her forehead, slightly embarrassed by the fact Bethany was leaning to one side, checking him out from behind, her lips curled in an 'O'. "I have heard people talking about this event all week. I thought I would come out and see what the fuss was all about."

"Are you enjoying it?" she asked, attempting to stave off her friend with the movement of her eyes.

"I truly am! I wasn't sure what to expect here in the States, but I find myself rather pleasantly surprised by the whole affair. It's quite charming in its own way."

"Cassie loves Halloween," Bethany blurted out. "She is all about the witchy stuff."

"Is that right?" His interest was genuinely piqued.

"I grew up in Salem." Cassie shrugged. "It's kind of hard to avoid it, but I do find it all extremely fascinating, especially from a scholarly perspective. I am not a practicing witch or anything—not that there is anything wrong with that."

"I must confess," he leaned towards her, "that makes two of us. I have recently developed a keen interest in the occult, as well. I have even begun to amass a small collection of literature on the subject, along with a few rare artifacts. You are welcome to see them for yourself or borrow any of the books I have if you like."

"Thank you! That is very kind of you. I would love to see what you have."

Bethany's face lit up like a Christmas tree watching the pair. "Cassie and I were just about to get our fortunes told. Would you like to join us?"

"Actually, I would, if I am not imposing, that is. I wouldn't want to interrupt your day of fun, but I find the concept intriguing and would be extremely interested in hearing what the future holds for my best student."

Cassie tucked her hair behind her ear and blushed. "Surely, I am not your best student!"

"Ah, you underestimate yourself. Your grades are excellent, your reputation among the faculty is impeccable, and you are one of the few pupils in my classes who is *majoring* in archeology." He flashed a warm smile. "I think you will do our field proud."

Bethany slipped her arm through his. "Well, let's go find out what the future holds, shall we?"

"Indeed!" Thomas extended his other arm for Cassie, which she accepted, and the three were off.

The fortune teller's tent they chose was swathed in rich, vibrant fabrics. A woven rug blanketed the ground and a small table rested in the center, low to the floor, the ensemble completed with a crystal ball. The smell of incense hung heavily in the air. Pillows were placed for seats and a rustic sign identified the mystic's name as 'Tallulah'.

"Do you wish to know your destiny?" asked the spiritualist, her words drawn out with a noticeable Eastern European accent. The woman, who could have been no more than forty, was dressed for the occasion, complete with long, full skirts, her lengthy, curly hair pushed back with a red wrap. It was anyone's guess as to whether she was an actual psychic or just an actress playing the part for the weekend.

"Yes!" Bethany pulled Cassie over and forced her to sit down at the table. "Cassie wants to know where to find a *real* man..." her eyes darted to the professor, who was standing with his arms folded, appearing more than a little amused by the situation, "who is NOT a college boy. She's had enough of them."

"Well, let's see what the fates have to say," replied Tallulah and took her by the hand, flipping it over so her palm was up.

"I think I have sworn off men," she whispered. "Maybe just a general reading would be more in order."

"Smart girl!" the woman responded with a wink. "Let's just see what comes up, shall we?" Concentrating, she stroked Cassie's hand a few times before focusing on the area intently, her jingling bracelets the only sound to be heard in the tent. "You have a bright future ahead of you," she said in a low, hypnotic voice. "I see here you will be very successful in your chosen field, being recognized with many awards. You will have the potential to make a great deal of money. Your love of the work will be what actually drives and fulfills you, but I see something else that is most unusual…" she paused, and furrowed her brow as she looked closer, "you also have the definitive mark of a witch, which means you carry the blood of an extremely powerful sorceress."

Cassie chuckled. "Hardly! My mother is an elementary school teacher, and my father is a factory worker. They never miss a Sunday morning church service."

"No, this goes back much further than that, by many generations." Tallulah looked up, a peculiar expression on her face. "You have a secret you have never told anyone—a gift bestowed upon you by your ancestors, yet you hide it from the world because you fear no one will understand. My dear, you are a very special young woman. You have no idea the power you possess!"

Cassie tensed and jerked her hand back as if she had been burned.

"*Do* you have a secret?" asked Bethany, giddy at the possibility. She also noticed Thomas's seemingly keen interest in her reply.

"Like I could keep one from you," she scoffed, nervously. Getting up, she moved quickly from the spot. "I believe it is your turn, Bethany."

The spiritualist's gaze remained focused on her while she and Bethany switched places.

Holding out her hand and wiggling her fingers, Bethany asked, "When will I meet Mr. Right?"

Tallulah, still staring at Cassie, reluctantly turned her attention to her next read. Clearing her throat and her mind, she took Bethany's hand and began to search the lines. "I see a handsome man in your near future. You will be meeting him any day now." Her face twisted, darkened, and she let out a burdened sigh.

"You will become heavily involved with him in the next three months, and all will seem to be going well, but his intentions are not what they seem. He will have ulterior motives and you must be careful of him, or he will cause you great heartache and pain."

"Oh!" Bethany made a face. "Okay, so the next guy is a dud. What about the one after him?"

Tallulah forced a smile and patted her hand. "While many things in a person's life are etched in stone, decided before they are even born, I am afraid, for you, this is one of those things that is not. Our free will gives us the power to create multiple outcomes and, especially in your case, the decisions you make regarding this man will determine your entire future. Tread carefully, sweet girl, and be cautious of the next man's attention, for he may cost you all you hold dear."

"I think I deserve a refund," Bethany jeered once they were outside, shaking her hands like a Magic Eight Ball, hoping to change the outcome. "That wasn't much of a fortune."

"I wouldn't put too much faith in it," said Thomas. "Most of these people are known charlatans looking to turn a quick coin. Don't give it a second thought."

"Maybe you're right, unless Cassie is holding out on us. Are you?"

"You and I have lived together since freshman year. What could I possibly be hiding that you wouldn't know anything about? As a matter of fact, I am fairly certain you can tell me what color underwear I'm wearing right at this exact moment."

"Of course! It's Saturday! They're red. Okay, we're going to chalk that reading up to being a bunch of nonsense. Who's hungry?"

Cassie breathed a sigh of relief when Bethany chose to let it go. The truth was—she did have a secret; one she had never told another soul. On her thirteenth birthday, she had been visited in her dreams by a woman claiming to be her great-grandmother. She was told she would be coming into an extraordinary gift—the ability to hold an item and garner visions from it. It would enable her to get rare glimpses into the past and serve her well in the future. Before her departure, the woman gave Cassie instructions on how to use and control it, as well as a stern warning—do not tell others, including her parents. Those who loved her would not understand and those who did not would try to find a way to exploit it for their own nefarious purposes.

"Blast it all!" Thomas patted the back pockets of his jeans. "I seem to be missing my phone. I think I may have dropped it when we stepped inside the tent. If you will excuse me for a moment, I will go check and be right back. Wait for me?"

"Of course," assured Cassie.

"He really is hot!" whispered Bethany as he walked away, appreciating the view.

"I guess so?"

"I wonder if *I* can get some extra credit," Bethany pondered aloud.

"Considering you are not in his class?"

"Maybe I can get *you* some extra credit!" She slung her arm around Cassie's shoulder. "After all, what are friends for?"

They waited, giggling until he reappeared.

"Found it!" he called out, holding it up as he came over to rejoin them. "So, what's good to eat around here? I am starving!"

"Miss Summers, I am glad I ran into you," he said as they sat down at a picnic table with their corn dogs and fries in hand. Thomas seemed to be examining the breaded concoction trying to figure out how best to approach it. Setting the container aside, he wiped his hands on a napkin and rested his forearms against the table's edge. "I have been meaning to speak with you but have been unable to catch you after class. I am completely overwhelmed and in desperate need of a teaching assistant. Unfortunately, it's a thankless job, one that would require you to spend a great deal of time in my office," Bethany's lips curled slightly up as he continued, "but it does pay a generous stipend and comes with a glowing letter of recommendation written to anyone you would like me to address it to. It will also allow you unfettered access to the college's private library collections and donors, who are good connections to have in the archaeology field. If you are interested, I would love to offer it to you."

"That's very tempting," replied Cassie, wiping a spot of mustard from her chin.

"I hear a 'but' coming on."

Bethany interjected before she could finish. "'But' nothing, she will take it and if she needs help, I will volunteer my services at no additional charge."

"Two assistants for the price of one? That sounds like a bargain to me!" Thomas looked to Cassie who was now glaring at her roommate. "Well? What do you say?"

Shrugging, Cassie shook her head and chuckled. "Well, I guess it's a 'yes'."

"Splendid! You can start on Monday."

The trio spent the rest of the day together, enjoying the festival and getting to know each other better. After a great deal of coaxing, they were even able to convince a somewhat reluctant Thomas to join them in a photo booth for a few silly snapshots to commemorate the momentous occasion.

Thirteen years later:

Cassie sat on the plane staring at the worn film strip she had carried in her leather journal with her since that day and smiled. Popping a Dramamine in her mouth, her eyes drifted to the window, the night sky becoming an inky backdrop to the memories that replayed in her mind.

That had been the beginning of a wonderful friendship. The three found themselves spending more and more time together over the following months. Thomas was a wonderful cook and often invited them over for dinner; the girls made sure to show him all their little college town had to offer. The trio cheerfully celebrated the good days and comforted each other on the lousy ones.

Thomas had been the bearer of the bad news on that dreadful day. Showing up on her doorstep, disheveled and visibly upset, he had explained how he was in the administrative office when the police came to the campus searching for information regarding Bethany's next of kin. After telling them he knew her personally, they told him about the accident and asked him to visit the scene to identify what was left of her

car. Thomas had also been her rock, the one who
caught her when she collapsed that day, holding her as
she inevitably fell apart, patiently drying her endless
flow of tears as they grieved together. As Cassie's
heart shattered, her steadfast savior jumped in to take
control of the situation. He made all the necessary
phone calls, dealt with the authorities, handled all the
funeral arrangements with her parents, and even flew
to Ohio with her for the service, remaining constantly
by her side throughout the hardest day of her life.
Attending the service for her best friend had been bad
enough, but to know there hadn't been anything left of
her to say goodbye to had been an unbearably cruel
twist of fate. In the middle of the night, less than a
week later after they returned from the service, he had
somehow sensed her plummet and felt her near the
edge of the abyss of the emptiness overwhelming her
mind, body, and soul. Submerged in a stunning
amount of grief and struggling to do something as
simple as taking her next breath, he had found her
curled in the fetal position, sobbing uncontrollably on
the bathroom floor. Sitting with his back against the
wall, he had gathered her up and pulled her onto his
chest, rocking and soothing her until the sun came up

and she gave in, surrendering to the sleep her body desperately needed.

In the days that followed, his concern for her mental and physical wellbeing had led to an invitation to stay at his home —and eventually into his bed—offering Cassie the only respite she could find from the storm uncontrollably raging within.

Bethany's death from a fiery car accident six months after the day that picture had been taken was the single worst thing that had ever happened to her, and she still felt the agony of it to this very day.

Cassie had not seen Thomas in person since the day she had graduated from college, four weeks after the funeral. He had unexpectedly been called back to London on urgent family business by his mother, and the night of the graduation ceremony was the last one they had spent together. In the wee hours of the morning, with the dawn rapidly approaching, they lay entangled in each other's arms speaking of their future together and promising to make time for one another.

As it often does, life had gotten in the way of their softly spoken desires and dreams, and their communication over the years had become less frequent—having dwindled to only one or two brief phone calls a year on special occasions, a monthly email to mention where one was working at the time, and finally a yearly Christmas card.

Cassie had, however, dropped everything when she received his peculiarly worded email two weeks ago asking for her assistance. There seemed to be some urgency to the matter, and though the details were a little vague, she could tell from reading between the lines, he was pleading for her help. Thomas had been there for her when she needed him the most, and she would be damned if she wouldn't return the favor.

"Did that come from one of those old-timey photo booths?" the man next to her asked, his remarkably golden eyes having wandered over. Lost in her thoughts, she had not even noticed he was there until he spoke. That was, in itself, odd, especially given her attention to even the smallest details. He was a striking older gentleman, with neatly trimmed salt and pepper hair and a beard wearing a long kilt. He spoke with a Scottish accent. An unusual sense of warmth and friendliness rolled off him.

"Yes, it is, but it was taken a while back."

"May I?"

Cassie handed it over.

The man smiled as he examined it closer. "It looks like it was indeed a delightful day."

"It was. That was taken at a Halloween festival a few years ago when I was in college."

"Is this young lady a good friend of yers?" He handed it back.

"She was—unfortunately she passed away shortly after this was taken."

"That's a shame, lass. I'm verra sorry to hear it," he patted her hand comfortingly, "but at least ye have yer memories. Fortunately, no one can ever take those away from ye."

"Yeah," she said, her eyes becoming watery. "I do have those."

"What about the man there?"

Cassie turned her head and discreetly wiped away a tear. "Another old friend, who I am actually on my way to meet now. He needs some help with his work."

"Is that right? What sort of profession might he be in?"

"He and I are both archaeologists."

"Ah, archaeologists! Ye are the ones who dig up all the old things!"

Cassie smirked. "Essentially—that's it in a nutshell."

The man tapped his chin. "There is an old saying I seem to recall—something about letting sleeping dogs lie, ye know? Perhaps, some things are better left buried where they are."

"Where's the fun in that?" she teased.

He leaned in closer. "I am all for stirring up a bit of trouble every now and again, and if I am being completely honest, I actually enjoy it far more than I should, but I am also about not biting off more than I can chew. It makes for a quieter life, ye know—and a longer one, at that."

Cassie stared straight ahead and gnawed on her lip, as she pondered her response. "If I am being completely honest," she finally said, "if my life were any quieter, I would be the one being dug up. I live the most boring life on the planet."

The old man laughed. "Well, ye never know when that might change, lass." He held out his hand, sporting a mischievous grin. "I am Finn, by the way, and I am pleased to make yer acquaintance."

"It's very nice to meet you, Finn. I am Cassie Summers."

"Ah Cassie, the pleasure is all mine." He reached into his coat and produced a flask. Removing the top, he drank down quite a bit before offering it to her.

"You're trouble, aren't you, Finn? You better hope that flight attendant doesn't catch you with that." She glanced over her shoulder, smirking, before accepting it and having a quick nip for herself. "They will throw us both into the ocean."

"It's alright, I am full of plenty of hot air —enough, in fact, to make us both just float away to some far away magical place where flight attendants and dull folks dare not tread," he said with a delightful chuckle, encouraging her to have some more. "So, this fellow ye are going to meet, is he an old flame by chance?"

"For a little while, a very long time ago," she shrugged, "but I haven't seen him in years."

"Hoping to pick up where ye left off?"

"I haven't really thought about it," she handed the flask back, "but, you never know, I suppose."

"Ye, lass, can do a great deal better," he remarked quietly.

If she hadn't known better, she could have sworn there was a slight tinge of disgust in his tone. Cassie narrowed her eyes at the older man. "Oh, you think so, huh?"

"Oh, I know so!" He nudged her shoulder with his, a twinkle in his eye. "How do you feel about older men in kilts with Scottish accents?"

She burst into laughter. "I have a feeling I wouldn't be able to keep up with you!"

"Oh, my dear, ye might be right about that, but ye would certainly have a great deal of fun trying!"

The two shared his seemingly bottomless contraband flask, along with a great deal of delightfully meaningless conversation over the remaining hours of the flight. Shortly before landing, Finn excused himself but never returned.

As she exited the plane, she stopped one of the airline stewardesses and asked about the gentleman.

"I am sorry, I am afraid I don't know who you are referring to. No one booked the seat next to yours."

"Surely you saw him. He was hard to miss—a handsome older gentleman, salt and pepper hair, Scottish accent?"

"No, I am afraid not. Have a lovely day," she replied, urging her along by looking to the person behind her.

"Huh!"

Now more curious than anything, Cassie kept an eye on the passengers as they departed the plane, but Finn seemed to have disappeared into thin air.

"Take care, Finn, wherever you are—or maybe I should call you D. B. Cooper," she muttered, walking towards the rental car booth. By the time she gathered her things and got on the road, she had begun to wonder if her traveling companion had been a figment of a Dramamine-induced dream, the details already beginning to fade away.

2

CHAPTER TWO

2020

North Elmham in the UK

"Welcome to North Elmham!" announced the cheery young innkeeper as she appeared around the corner, out of nowhere, with a plate of freshly baked chocolate scones in hand. "You must be Dr. Summers!"

"I am," she replied, softly closing the door behind her, "but please, call me Cassie." Her eyes drifted to the plate of pastries, her stomach grumbling at the sight. "Those look delicious!"

"Help yourself!" The woman presented the dish with a smile. "I am sure you are famished. Those damn airlines and their ridiculous money-saving cutbacks will starve a poor girl to death these days. I'm Jessie

Reed, by the way, the owner of this place, and I have been expecting you."

"But I'm a day early!" Cassie reached for the largest scone on top and took a bite, letting out a delightful moan. Her taste buds rejoiced at the still-warm chocolate, pleasantly surprised and pleased to receive something that didn't come from a plastic wrapper for a change.

"I had a hunch you might be, and my feelings are not usually wrong, so your room is all set up."

"That's great! Thank you so much. I'm looking forward to a good night's sleep." Cassie's attention turned to her surroundings. "The pictures on the website don't do this place justice," she remarked, struggling to catch the crumbs in her hand as she ventured further inside, taking in the intricate details of the grand fireplace on the far wall of the library. "The pattern and wear of the stonework outside suggest early eighteenth century," her eyes went up and followed an extended, exposed center beam, "but I would say parts of it are much, much older. If I had to venture a guess, I would estimate the early 1600s."

"It seems you are well-versed in your craft!" Jessie said with a grin. "This place has been around forever and added onto a little bit at a time over the years. Thankfully, my grandparents had the foresight to add indoor plumbing early on. It came in handy when I decided to turn it into an inn after I inherited it a few years ago." Jessie glanced towards the door. "Where's your luggage?"

Cassie turned sightly and shrugged up one shoulder, showing off her trusty leather backpack. "This is it, other than my tools, which are in the trunk of my rental car. I tend to travel rather lightly since I'm usually roughing it in a tent without indoor plumbing. Most dig sites don't have nice places like this nearby. I guess I just got lucky this time."

Cassie Summers had quickly risen through the ranks as one of the top archaeologists in her field, especially when it came to deciphering the mysteries of the unknown. The discovery she was there for was only a few miles up the road.

"Well, it seems our sleepy little town is having its fifteen minutes of fame." Jessie motioned her towards the stairs. "Everyone is talking about it. It's been the hottest topic in town for days. There are even whispers of the entire project being 'cursed'. Personally, I don't see what all the fuss is about."

Cassie popped the final morsel into her mouth and followed her hostess. "That's what I'm here to find out."

The following morning, Cassie got directions from Jessie and drove over to the work site. Opening the door, she got out and looked around at the partially wooded lot with a tent pitched at the entrance, noting the area around it had been roped off. Several people were busy using sieves to sift through the soil, while others were measuring and marking off lines with twine. A couple of security guards were hanging out in a trailer that had been brought in, presumably to keep the area secure at night. After checking in with them, Cassie glanced towards the tent to see a man determinedly headed in her direction—and one she would have recognized anywhere.

"Cassie!" Thomas called out with a wave of a hand and a broad smile on his face. "You're one day sooner than I expected!"

"I caught an earlier flight!"

The two met halfway and warmly embraced, taking the time to look each other over.

"It's good to see you, Thomas! It seems the private sector agrees with you after all!"

"Well, it definitely agrees with my bank account," he teased. "And look at you! My God, you look wonderful, as always! I wish you had called to let me know your arrival had been moved up. I wanted to personally welcome you at the airport."

"Forget it! I got in late and went straight to bed."

Thomas now worked as a private consultant, having started his own business a few years earlier, and his company was called in to confer whenever artifacts turned up unexpectedly at construction sites. He had gained a good reputation as one of the few in the trade and was extremely well-respected among his colleagues in the archaeological community.

Placing his arm around her shoulders, he guided her inside. "God, how I've missed you! It has been far too long since we last saw each other. I can't thank you enough for dropping everything to answer my call!"

"I'm sorry it took me so long to get here. I was finishing up a dig in Arizona and had quite a few loose ends to wrap up before I could leave."

"Well, you are here now and that is all that matters," he said with an affectionate grin. "And once I have filled you in, I have a feeling you will be glad you came."

Cassie's eyes swept over the scattered tables inside the tent. "So, don't keep me in suspense! Let me have all the juicy details."

Thomas escorted her to the makeshift desk near the back, covered with weathered maps, hand-scribbled notes, and plenty of dirt. Offering her a rickety chair, he produced a bottle of whisky from a battered filing cabinet and poured two glasses.

"A local developer bought this land with the intention of putting up a strip mall, but as soon as they started acting on his plans a few weeks ago, things started to go downhill. The foreman had a heart attack on his first day on the job and will be recovering for the foreseeable future. A mysterious flu bug overtook half the crew three days in, and one week later, there was the mysterious accident with the excavator where the arm snapped completely in half with its third lift of soil, something I have never once even heard of happening. That's when things got interesting."

"*That's* when things got interesting?" she asked, taking a sip from the glass.

"Indeed! My team was called in when a set of remains was discovered in that final scoop that broke the machine. Not knowing anything about what we were dealing with, of course, I shut everything down, cordoned off the area, and started looking into the matter."

"And?"

"So far, we have uncovered what appears to be a perfectly circular perimeter about six meters across, along with eleven sets of completely intact remains inside of it."

Cassie's shoulders slumped, her enthusiasm suddenly waning. "You called me in for a cemetery? I didn't need to fly halfway around the world to see one of those, even if you are about to tell me you are convinced their spirits are haunting the grounds. I know it's almost Halloween, and I'm a sucker for that kind of thing, but come on, Thomas! Give me a break!"

He grinned. "A plain old burial site is exactly what I thought it was—at first. I was just about to suggest they fill it back in, leave the dead to rest in peace, and build on the other side of the property—until I noticed it."

"Noticed what?"

"The first, of course, had been disturbed, but as the others were unearthed…" Thomas slid a few photographs over in front of her, marked where the remains had been found in the area, "their bodies were not placed as they would have been with normal interments. There are no coffins, not even a fragment of one, and each skeleton found so far has been laid head to toe, as if in a specific pattern, following the curve. There is also evidence this land was scorched at about the same time."

"So, it is a mass burial site," she said dismissively. "You know as well as I do when things like the plague and famine come around and bodies are piling up faster than the gravediggers can shovel, people tend to forget about ceremonies and formalities, and with good reason."

"Fair enough," he smirked and reached for a plastic bag, which he placed in front of her, "and an assessment I would normally agree with if *these* had not been mixed in with the bones. It makes the pattern a little more curious, even you will have to admit."

Cutting her eyes at him, Cassie snatched the bag from his hand and held it up for a closer inspection rather unenthusiastically. Her demeanor suddenly transformed when it registered what she held. "Rune stones?" She flipped it over to examine the details more closely. "On the bodies?"

"We have found them with every single one so far and there is reason to believe there are even more to uncover."

"What's the history of this area?" she asked and straightened up, giving Thomas her full attention.

"You tell me," he replied rather smugly and paused to sip from his glass. "You *are* staying at a place aptly named 'The Witch's Globe'." Leaning across the table, he asked, "Tell me—have I managed to pique the interest of the great Dr. Cassie Summers?"

"Maybe?"

"I think I will win you over once you get a good look at the fully laid out site. You have to see it to truly appreciate it."

A slow smile spread across her face. "Well, since I am already here!"

3

CHAPTER THREE

"Do you still remember how to get your hands dirty, or have you gotten spoiled sitting behind a desk?" Cassie goaded, pulling her hair back in a ponytail and dipping her head in the direction of his bright-white button-down shirt.

Standing with his hands resting on his hips, Thomas followed her gaze downward, chuckling when he caught her meaning. "Oh! I had an early meeting with the owner of the property this morning. Needless to say, he wasn't very happy and took his sweet time expressing his dissatisfaction with the progress of his project. I had intended to go back home and change but the morning got away from me." Swirling his finger in the air above his head, he added, "Never fear, I always keep a spare work shirt in my truck."

"You live here?"

"No, my main home is still in London, but I do have a small place on the water close by where I come to fish when I need to get away. It beats staying in a tent any day. I will admit, I just don't enjoy the 'roughing it' part as much as I used to. Inevitably, your knees always begin to ache from the years of working in these blasted holes. Trust me, the day will come when you will learn to appreciate the little luxuries like memory foam mattresses and hot tubs of bath water. The cold, hard ground just doesn't hold its appeal like it used to."

The corners of her eyes crinkled with amusement. "You're just getting soft in your old age!"

"Yes, you're probably right!" he willingly admitted, touching her arm as he passed by. "Let me go grab my work clothes!"

Cassie regarded him as he exited the tent. The truth was—*nothing* had gone soft on that man. Thomas Armstrong was in much better shape than he had ever been in college, and Cassie had certainly taken notice. Discretely watching him walk away, she took a moment to appreciate the crisp white collared shirt he wore, thin enough to show off his well-toned shoulders and biceps. It paired nicely with the snugly tailored pair of trousers he wore.

"So, how's life been treating you?" he asked when he returned, buttoning up the tan shirt he now wore. "What have you been up to besides showing up scholars and piling up accolades?"

"You know I don't care anything about that," she replied, pretending to be interested in a map of the town on the table. "I just love the work and seeing the world."

"You really should use some of that clout to land yourself a cushy office job with an overworked air-conditioner and a fat paycheck. If I have one piece of advice to offer as your former advisor, it is to get out of the trenches *before* your body starts to protest."

"How else am I going to get my exercise?" Cassie waved him off. "And what would I do with all that money?"

"Buy yourself a house to store all those awards in?" He stroked his chin as a sudden thought occurred to him. "Are you still renting that God-awful tiny apartment in California?"

"I love my little apartment!" she objected. "It's very comfy and cozy!"

Thomas crossed his arms. "Do you still have to fold the bed up into the wall to get into the kitchen?"

"I can't cook and sleep at the same time anyway!" Cassie rolled her eyes. "Besides, it's just me and I'm never there anyway. What about you? Entertaining the Queen at your family's home in London?"

"Not there, but she did have me over for a spot of tea a couple of months ago to thank me for some work I did with the British Museum."

Shaking her head, she groaned. "You charm the royals; I will stick to digging in the trenches. They would hate me anyway because I think milk in tea is disgusting. I wouldn't know which spoon to stir with anyway."

Thomas came over and put his arm around her shoulders. "I think you would fit in perfectly," he squeezed, "and I think they would love you as much as I do." Rubbing her upper limb, he leaned in and whispered, "I have missed you, Cassie."

"I've missed you too, Thomas."

And she had, more than she realized. At that moment, with his arm around her and his face close to hers, all felt right in the world.

"Come on!" He guided her towards the dig site. "I can't wait to show you what we've found!"

Cassie and Thomas emerged from the back of the tent to where the excavation was well underway. Approaching the first hole, the two dusty men working on it stepped back to reveal a pit about three feet deep, and in it, the outline of a skull with the bones of a hand outstretched to one side. Cassie stepped around the men and peered down.

"The first one that was uncovered was just about here," Thomas explained, pointing to a spot of Earth that had been dug out with a machine. "If you will notice, the head looks as if it might have been placed just at the feet of this other one."

"Alright!" mumbled Cassie as she stared down, making a mental note of the unusual placement of the hands.

Thomas pressed his hand to the small of her back and led her to the next pit covered with a tarp. Pulling it aside, she could see this set of remains was on its

side placed in the same way. Cassie grew even more
curious as the tour continued, finding each skeleton
arranged in a consistent position, covered with rune
stones, and with one other thing in common—each
had all five fingers pointing in the same direction.

"What's up with these rune stones?" she asked.

"Each set of remains seems to have their own
collection, because each is of its suit, but is dissimilar
in its appearance from the next. That would be
consistent if each individual had his or her own set.
As you well know, that would have been a very
personal thing to the holder, but the one thing they do
all have in common is that the Algiz stone, the symbol
for protection, is placed in every palm."

"That's a little odd," she muttered.

"Indeed!"

Curiously, Cassie stopped and rotated around, taking
in the scene, and forming a broader picture in her
mind. "Have you run this over with ground-
penetrating radar?"

"Of course!" He pointed to where a section was
cordoned off. "We have flagged all the spots where
the ground has been disturbed at the same depth and
there are two areas left." Cassie's eyes swept the

vicinity to see a few men digging in those two segments.

"So, if the pattern holds, it forms a perfect circle?"

"Exactly! And given what we have uncovered thus far, it would also essentially be an *unbroken* circle."

It was then that something peculiar caught Cassie's eye. In the dead center of the bodies was a grassless, barren blackened spot where nothing grew. She made her way over to it, toeing the ground with her shoe. "Did you scan here?"

"We did!" Thomas nodded. "It was inconclusive. I thought it best to work from the outside in, but if I am being completely honest, I wanted to wait until you were here. I have a strange feeling there is something of great importance down there, and I wanted another expert here to back me up."

Once the bigger picture came together in her mind, Cassie audibly gasped, turning to Thomas, a perplexed expression on her face.

"Curious now?" he asked.

Her face split into a grin. "You better believe it!"

"I HAVE REMAINS!" called out one of the men as he stood on the top rung of the ladder from the twelfth hole waving his bandana. Cassie and Thomas rushed over and quickly descended into the ground where they found the tip of a toe bone emerging from the soil. Cassie reached for her trusty, dusty brush in her back pocket. Touching the bristle to the bone, she paused when the ground beneath them shifted slightly. Drawing back, she looked over her shoulder. "Did you feel something?"

"I certainly did!" Thomas surveyed the space around them, at a loss as to what could have caused it. "What the hell was that?"

Shrugging, she turned her attention back to the foot at hand. As the brush touched the bone, they felt the strange movement once again, only this time it was much stronger and accompanied by an eerie sound.

Instincts kicking in, Thomas firmly grasped Cassie by the arm. "Up the ladder!" he ordered and urged her forward, following closely behind. As soon as they were out of the pit, the barely unearthed skeleton began to shake, emerging from the soil, and rising as if of its own accord.

"What the actual fuck?" muttered Cassie, her eyes wide with disbelief as the dark eyes of a hundred toads suddenly materialized from beneath the dirt. Digging their way free, they overflowed the gravesite, bringing the remains to the top with them. Within moments, the wart-covered creatures blasted the air with their ear-piercing croaks, leaving the entire excavation site teeming with their presence. The uninvited guests sent the workers scrambling from inside the circle into the safety of the shelter.

Thomas shielded Cassie with his body and hurried her into the tent where the others had already gathered, securing the flaps behind them to keep the undesirable amphibians at bay.

"That's it!" exclaimed one of the workers and threw his hat to the ground. "This is the final straw. I am sorry, Thomas, but someone is trying to tell us we should not be digging here! I, for one, cannot continue to work this site!"

Thomas turned to face him, his eyes imploring him to reconsider. "Jim! You have been by my side for eight years! You were here when I started this company and now, you're just going to walk out on me, just like that?"

"I am on THIS job. It's just not worth the money!"

"Over a few frogs?" questioned a rather confused Cassie.

"A few frogs?" A young woman wearing a cross around her neck glanced nervously over her shoulder and scoffed. "What about last week when we came in to find locusts covering our tools? That's biblical plague stuff! I'm not about pissing off the 'big guy'! As a matter of fact, I'm heading to church as soon as these little green monsters let me out of here, and I am begging forgiveness for whatever I did to get on His bad side. I would advise the rest of you to do the same."

"Let's not forget to mention the freak hailstorm two days after that!" added another. "I'm with Jim! I never believed in curses before, but I am starting to wonder. I think it's a good time for me to use some of that built-up vacation time."

The crowd started to confer among themselves, all seemingly drawing the same conclusion.

"Wait! Is ANYONE planning on finishing this excavation?" queried Thomas as he tried to settle them down. "This is what we do! Uncovering history is our job!"

"Yeah, but we would like to uncover it, not become a part of it by getting our names carved on a memorial stone because we died for it."

When the crowd fell silent, Thomas shook his head in defeat. "Fair enough! I will admit, this has been the most difficult excavation I've ever been a part of, but I also believe it is worth it. The work will continue, but it's up to each of you individually if you want to be a part of it. I won't fault anyone for leaving if you think it is in your best interest, and you will be paid for the full week regardless. If you stay, however, I will triple your wages for the remainder of the time we are here."

The frog's songs outside eventually began to die down and the workers continued to debate among themselves as each started to make their own decision known.

An hour later, the company was down to six people. Thomas shook the hands of the ones who remained and thanked them profusely before sending them back to work.

"Has it been as bad as all that?" Cassie asked once they were alone.

Thomas raked his hair back and sat down in the nearest chair, perching his elbows on his knees, the stress of the dig showing on his face. "I hate to say it, but it has! In addition to the locusts, the toads, and the hailstorms, I was already down to a skeleton crew, no pun intended, because three of my best people have been injured in freak, on-the-job accidents. I can't afford to lose anyone else. I need help, now more than ever."

Cassie rubbed his shoulders. "Well, I am not going anywhere, and I am not afraid of a little hard work, not to mention the fact that I hear frog legs are a delicacy in Slovenia. Maybe we can make a little cash on the side while we're at it."

He managed a chuckle, reaching up and covering her hand with his. "Thank you, Cassie! I knew I could count on you."

She rested her chin on the top of his head and hugged him from behind. "You know I will always be here for you, Thomas!"

Cassie and Thomas spent the rest of the day cleaning out the toad-infested grave while the others who remained behind worked on the thirteenth. She made her way back to the inn well after dark, covered from head to toe in dirt and reeking of stagnant pond water.

"Good Lord!" exclaimed Jessie and reached for a towel as Cassie tried to quietly slip in through the back kitchen door. "Did you fall head-first into a six-foot-deep mud hole?"

"More like a toad hole," she replied and gratefully accepted the towel, using it to scrub the dirt from her face.

"Toads?" Jessie blinked hard before bursting into laughter. "What in the world?"

"Yeah, it was the weirdest thing. I have never seen so many of them in one place before. There had to have been hundreds of them, and they were so stinking loud!"

"How odd! I've lived here all my life and I can count on one hand how many times I've seen one." Jessie pointed to the sink as she placed a steaming bowl of food on the counter. "Wash up and sit down. You look hungry."

"What did you make?" Cassie scrubbed her hands, the wonderful smell making her mouth water.

"Just a little beef stew I made too much of for myself. Good thing you are here so it doesn't go to waste."

"You are going to spoil me," she said as she took a seat.

"Wine or beer?"

"Beer!"

Jessie smiled, taking two bottles from the fridge and removing the caps. "A girl after my own heart!"

"God, this is so good!" Cassie raved after taking a bite of the stew. "Where did you learn to cook like this?"

"My mother and grandmother were pretty good in the kitchen! They taught me everything they knew, along with a few secret recipes that have been passed down for generations. I've found cooking to be extremely relaxing for me and a great deal cheaper than therapy. I do like to watch people enjoy my food." She leaned one hand on the counter and took a sip of her beer. "I take it you aren't much of a cook?"

"No, not living on the road. I mean, the excavation teams get together at night and do a lot of grilling, but I tend to keep to myself. Depending on where I'm working, I either eat a lot of takeout or a bunch of freeze-dried stuff that needs a great deal of water to make it edible. I do pack a lot of snacks though, just to keep my sweet tooth happy."

"It sounds like a lonely life."

"It's not so bad. I can remember a time in my life when being alone made me feel like I was suffocating." That night on the bathroom floor flashed briefly in her mind, and she shook it off. "But I have learned to embrace the solitude." Cassie finished her bowl. "Thank you so much for this. It was delicious and it hit the spot, especially after today. Now I just need to get a little sleep and I will be as good as new."

Jessie grabbed another beer from the refrigerator, turned, and rested her forearms on the counter. "Might I suggest a bath first, for the sake of my extremely expensive Egyptian cotton linens?" She slid the bottle over in front of her with one finger and grinned. "One for the tub! Consider it a gift, or a bribe—whichever keeps me from having to replace those stunningly beautiful bright white sheets!"

"Well, when you put it that way," Cassie seized the bottle and laughed, "consider me officially bribed. I will see you in the morning!"

4

CHAPTER FOUR

Two days later, Cassie and Thomas's initial conjectures were confirmed. Thirteen female corpses were indeed deliberately laid out to form a perfect circle, each one with a protection rune stone resting in its palm, pointing in the direction of the dead center.

The pair stood over the spot, contemplating the possibilities, giddy with anticipation. Figuring it was probably a long shot but worth a try, Cassie knelt and pressed her hand to the ground. She received no reading, needing instead to physically hold onto a specific item and focus for the magic to happen.

"Well, I guess there is only one way to find out what we are dealing with," she said rubbing her hands together excitedly before standing up and reaching for a nearby shovel. "Might as well get digging!"

"Whatever you say, Dr. Summers!" Thomas agreed.

Before she could turn the first bit of ground, an abrupt shot of frigid air blasted across the excavation site, toppling the makeshift tents erected over the graves, turning over wheelbarrows, and sending heavy, iron tools soaring through the air like helium-filled balloons. Laborers rushed to gather their items, but a static jolt charged the atmosphere, fierce enough to stand hair on end and turn day into night like the flick of a switch. Savage streaks of purple lightning illuminated the sky, and the stench of sulfur pervaded the air. A torrent of rain burst forth from the heavens, even though, moments before, there had not been a single cloud in the sky.

After rushing to secure the area, the workers sprinted to their cars and called it a day. Thomas and Cassie hurried to his truck and jumped inside, both laughing even though they were soaked and freezing from the rain.

"I don't know about you, but I think we have earned a hot meal and a few drinks," he said and started the engine. "There's a great pub just up the street. What do you say?"

"I say it sounds like a plan," she agreed.

After putting the truck in gear, Thomas eased up to the door of the trailer to let the security team know they were headed out for the rest of the evening.

"I know I haven't spent much time in the UK," she remarked as they pulled onto the main road, "but is this sort of thing normal? Do thunderstorms blow up out of nowhere like this, I mean?"

Reaching over, Thomas fiddled with the knob to turn on the heater. "It is a little late in the season for them, but it's not unheard of. Although, we usually do get a little more notice. This one certainly gave no indication it was brewing." He leaned over and lightly brushed the side of her thigh with the back of his hand, a grin on his face. "Who knows? Maybe this place *is* cursed after all!"

"Yeah, right!" she scoffed.

The dimly lit pub was a welcome sight for the waterlogged pair. A roaring fireplace crackled and popped along the far wall, creating a warm, inviting atmosphere. Locals huddled at the crowded bar, their lively conversation toning down and their eyes drifting to the newcomers. The two grabbed the booth closest to the hearth and settled in, away from the others, where they could have some privacy.

"So, tell me, what do you think is buried out there?" Thomas asked as the two enjoyed their Lagers while waiting for their supper.

"I'm not sure what you've stumbled on, but I am interested in finding out more about it," she paused and eyed him warily. "I'm also wondering exactly why you called me in on this. Most of the work had already been done by the time I arrived, and your people didn't quit on you until after I got here. So, Thomas, why don't you fess up and tell me what's really going on?"

"Maybe I just missed you!" he replied, his gaze locked solidly on hers.

Cassie's heart skipped a beat when he flashed a warm, sexy smile. Shaking her head, she indicated she wasn't buying what he was selling. But, if she were being honest, the thought of him missing her was one that pleased her more than she ever imagined it might. "Something tells me that isn't the reason you contacted me after all this time."

Thomas lowered his head and conceded with a smirk. "Alright, there is a little more to it, but I want the pleasure of seeing your face when the reality of it hits you. Indulge the old professor in me, if you will, and let's start with what we have already uncovered. Thirteen bodies in a circle, all facing inward and buried with protective rune stones, clearly pointing toward something in the middle. From an anthropological standpoint, what is it and why is it important?"

"Okay, I'll humor you and play along as your student, for old-time's sake." She leaned back in her seat and crossed her arms. "Just out of curiosity, have you carbon-dated the first set of remains?"

"Of course, I have! What kind of mediocre archaeologist do you take me for?" he teased and pulled out his phone, opened an email, and handed it to her.

"Late sixteenth century?" she questioned, skimming the results and handing it back to him, a curious expression on her face. "That would imply witch trials."

"Trials, no!" he corrected. "According to the research, the only documented witch trial activity in this particular area was carried out by two men you will have heard of—the famed 'witchfinder', Matthew Hopkins, and his associate, John Stearne —only they did most of their work around the year 1644. These remains are from more than fifty years earlier, long before they were even born."

"It wouldn't have been them anyway!" Cassie drummed her fingers on the table, cocking her head to one side. "There is no way any witch hunter worth their salt would have buried them this way. These women would have been burned, hanged, or dunked, and there was certainly no reason to place them in the formation they are in now. That alone would have been seen as sacrilegious or as an offering to the Devil himself but add the rune stones into the mix and the whole town would have been in an uproar—*if* they knew about it, that is."

"Which begs the question—*who* would have done such a thing?" he mused, waiting for her to draw the same conclusion he had already come to.

"Other witches!" she mumbled, the implications slamming into her as the pieces fell into place. "It was a secret ceremony of some sort, but carried out among themselves, using their own as part of the ritual—and a sizeable one at that!"

Thomas waggled his finger at her. "You always were my brightest pupil!"

"They must have considered it a high priority, especially since nothing like this has ever been documented, much less discovered, and to have actual tangible evidence…" Cassie chewed on her bottom lip, "well, this would change everything."

"Now, you see why I enlisted your help," he explained. "It wasn't too hard to figure out *who* did it, but what we need to know is the *what* and the *why*— and the best expert in the field for figuring out *those* types of mysteries is YOU!"

Cassie Summers had become THE expert in archaeology known for solving the mysteries that had stumped scholars for decades, having risen quickly through the ranks early on, all thanks to her secret visions. When a simple, unassuming Revolutionary War-era doll had been donated to a local museum, Cassie had been able to determine, and prove, that it had been used to smuggle medications into one of the prison camps. That was achieved when she easily demonstrated the secret trick to opening it, much to the astonishment of the attending experts. While working at a Civil War-era home excavation in South Carolina, the group had been shown an unusually shaped key by the owner that had been passed down through the generations. With it came a whole slew of speculations as to what it opened. Everyone who had ever visited the home had been stumped, including several leading museum specialists. As soon as Cassie took it in hand, she walked straight into the drawing-room, located a keyhole hidden in the stone hearth by a front stone, and inserted it to reveal a secret compartment. The inexplicable drawer held the original deed to the home, along with several historically significant documents, which the Smithsonian crawled on hands and knees to acquire.

She could name any number of instances where things like that had occurred and her 'gift' had come in quite handy, especially given her chosen line of work.

"If this is what I believe it to be," he continued, "it will be the find of the century," Thomas reached across and rested his hand gently on hers, "and something I can't imagine sharing with anyone other than you."

The offer in itself was quite tempting but adding the man sitting opposite her into the mix, made it even more enticing. When they had been together before, she had been young, vulnerable, and not in a good place. Even if he had stayed, there would have been little future for them.

But that had been a long time ago, and in the past few years, Cassie had found a certain amount of inner peace within herself, happy and confident in the woman she had become. Now that she had grown up, things were, and could be, much different.

Cassie looked down at his hand on hers and couldn't imagine wanting to be anywhere else at that moment, though she wasn't ready to admit it aloud. Instead, she said, "You know what a sucker I am for anything witchy! Count me in!"

After gorging themselves on fish and chips and several more beers, the topic of conversation shifted. Soon, they found themselves reminiscing about their college days.

"How are your folks?" he asked out of the blue.

A wistful expression crossed her face. Running the tip of her finger around the rim of her glass, she fought back a few tears. "Dad passed away three years ago from a massive stroke. Too many years of hard work took a toll on his body."

Wincing, he shifted in his seat and leaned forward. "Oh, Cassie, I am so sorry to hear that. You should have called me. I would have dropped everything and flown out to be with you if I had known."

She nodded and cleared her throat. "Mom is doing well, though. She's still teaching and won't even consider retiring. She claims the kids keep her young and I suppose she's not wrong."

"Your mother knows what's best for her. It's probably better she keeps herself occupied."

"Why haven't you settled down?" she asked, desperately wanting to change the subject.

Thomas shrugged. "I don't know, I suppose I' am just waiting for the right person to come along. I could ask the same of you!"

"I don't have time," she replied, brushing off his question. "I spend less than three weeks a year in that God-awful apartment you were giving me such a hard time about. I'm always on the road, and long-distance relationships never work out. You and I know that better than anyone."

He nodded understandingly. "Have you considered taking something a little more settled?"

"Like a nine-to-five job?" She laughed. "I wouldn't know how to act. Anyway, who would hire me?"

"You mean besides any museum in the world worth its salt? Wherever you choose to go would be lucky to have you. You know, I have connections and there's a lot to be said for working in a place with air conditioning and a nice retirement plan."

"You may have a point there," she conceded with a chuckle. "But you know how I like getting my hands dirty."

"Well then, come work with me! There isn't anything that would please me more, and believe me when I say, I have plenty to keep us both busy. I've recently been considering taking on a partner anyway. I can't think of anyone better suited for the role."

Cassie shook her head. "I don't know! That doesn't sound like me."

"Come on," he encouraged. "I will let you have the exclusive on all the dirty work, while I handle the business side of things. As a matter of fact, saying it aloud makes it sound like an even better plan."

"I think we should get through one dig at a time," she countered.

"Alright but keep it in the back of your mind and promise me you'll give it some serious thought."

"I will!"

And she would. The thought of having him back in her life was something she liked the idea of very much.

The storm had abated, and a multitude of stars filled the sky by the time Thomas drove Cassie back to the inn. Cracking the window, she inhaled the fresh, crisp odor of the fall rain mingling with a faint whiff of wood smoke from a nearby chimney and smiled. There was something about this time of year she loved more than any other. A sense of peace and contentment filled her.

"Look at that! It turned out to be a beautiful night," she remarked. "The view here is something else."

His eyes swept over her. "Yes, it certainly is."

Cassie was grateful for the darkness of the night sky when her cheeks flushed red from his words.

"You want to come in for a nightcap?" she asked when they pulled into the drive.

"I can think of nothing I would like more!"

She took him by the hand, leading the way inside and into the library. No one else was around, so they helped themselves to the tray of adult beverages that had been left on the side table.

"I owe you an apology," he said as she handed him a glass and joined him on the sofa.

"For what?"

Looking down into the amber liquid, he swished it around, pondering his words carefully. "For not living up to my promise to make time for you after we last saw each other. It's not that I didn't want to—I did, more than anything—but you were beginning your life anew and, after Bethany's death, I didn't want you to feel obligated to drag me along for the ride. You deserved a chance to move forward without a daily reminder of what happened every time you looked at me. Being the one who had to break that dreadful news to you, well—I couldn't help but feel like every time you saw my face, it made you think of that terrible day. I was wrong! I should have been there for you, but I wasn't, and I have regretted that fact every day since."

Cassie tucked her legs beneath her and turned to face him better. "Thomas, you have nothing to apologize for. I only have fond memories of our time together, and it was as much my fault as it was yours. There was so much loss and change at that time for me—I needed to be alone to pull myself together. After Bethany's death, my graduation, and your departure, I threw myself into my work to fill the void. I made time for nothing else, and it was better that way. Working eighteen hours a day was the one thing that kept me sane, and eventually, it deadened the pain into a dull ache." Her hand drifted over to rest on his upper thigh. "Please don't feel guilty for it. Things worked out for the best in the long run."

"Did they?" Leaning closer, their eyes met. "Not one day has gone by when I haven't thought about you and wondered what would have happened if I had not returned to London. You have no idea how much I wish I had handled the entire situation differently." Moving forward, his lips slowly found their way to hers. Hesitating, he waited for her response. Would it be an invitation for more or a kindhearted refusal?

Cassie did not attempt to hamper his actions, instead, she encouraged him to continue. The two were happily engrossed in one another—until the door loudly burst open and they were interrupted by a few boisterous guests wandering in, having already had quite a bit to drink.

"Oops!" they heard a woman say. "Wrong room! This one seems to already be occupied!" She laughed and stumbled back into the hall, into the arms of her mate.

Cassie and Thomas leaned into each other and grinned. The moment had been nice, but thanks to the interruption, it had passed.

"I should go," Thomas whispered reluctantly, taking the time to lovingly cup her face, committing each feature to memory.

"And I should get some rest," she begrudgingly concurred. "We have a big day ahead of us tomorrow."

Planting a final tender kiss on her forehead before he stood, he held onto her hand and said, "I look forward to continuing this later. Good night, Cassie, sleep well. You will be in my dreams."

"Good night, Thomas."

Due to a combination of the anticipation of what discovery they might make the next day, and the possibilities of where the sweet kiss they shared might lead, Cassie found herself tossing and turning, unable to sleep. Finally giving up, she balled the expensive Egyptian sheets up and angrily tossed them onto the floor out of frustration. Blowing the hair out of her face, she decided to just get dressed and head to the dig site early. On her way out, she found Jessie already in the kitchen cooking up a ton of food even though the sun had not yet risen.

"Good morning, Cassie! Did you sleep well?"

"I did!" Cassie lied, rubbing her eyes with her palms.

"Hungry?" she asked, plating a pan of cooked eggs and sausages.

"Truthfully? Starving!" Cassie pulled a chair up to the counter and Jessie placed it in front of her. Leaning forward, she inhaled the scrumptious smell and smiled. "You are doing a fine job of spoiling me! I won't be able to fit through the door before long."

"I take it you are not much of a breakfast eater." The inn hostess poured a glass of orange juice and slid it over in front of her.

"Just not used to all this home cooking," she replied and picked up her fork. "Especially, not as good as this. I have been all over the world and I can honestly say, yours is some of the best I have ever tasted. You really do have a knack for it."

Jessie beamed with pride. "Cooking is my therapy. It truly does relax me and help me forget my problems. I am always experimenting with new recipes and making entirely more food than any one person should, which by the way, you are welcome to at any time. I know your schedule is varied, but please feel free to help yourself anytime to whatever you find as often as you like. I want you to treat my home as your own while you are here."

"Thank you so much for everything." As Jessie moved to the sink to wash a pan, Cassie took a closer look at the counter. It was made with timber like the main beam running throughout the house she had noticed when she first arrived. "This wood is stunning!"

"Oh yes! We had a water leak a few years back and had to replace one of the walls from the original part of the house. It broke my heart to lose so much of it, but I was able to salvage enough to make that and put it to even better use, here where I would still be able to enjoy it daily. I have to say, I had no idea it would turn out as wonderfully as it did."

Jessie's back still turned and finding herself extremely curious, Cassie let her hand rest on the top, closing her eyes, silently requesting a vision. She was soon engulfed in one of an older woman from centuries earlier, happily singing as she tied bundles of fresh herbs and hung them to dry on the same piece of wood she was having her breakfast on. The image made her smile. The scene around her slowly faded away when Jessie stepped over, her face briefly replacing the older woman's, as she asked if she would like a slice of toasted bread.

"No, thank you. I think I have plenty," Cassie replied and dug in with her fork. "I am so taken with this place. Tell me, why did you name it 'The Witch's Globe', if you don't mind me asking?"

"Not at all. There have always been rumors about so-called 'witches' in the area, passed down over the years, and given all the interest in the paranormal these days, it just seemed like a good marketing ploy at the time. It's panned out for me."

"Fair enough!" Cassie sipped her juice. "Do you know any of the stories about the witches who were supposedly around here?"

"Why do you ask?"

"Just the archaeologist in me, I guess. I'm always interested in the local lore whenever I travel, mostly because I have found there always tends to be a hint of truth somewhere in every tall tale told."

"I have heard a few," Jessie used a towel to wipe away a few crumbs, "but there is always one story that comes to mind. It's about a woman named Millicent Davies. She was part of a coven who used their abilities to help the village prosper, but one day, Millicent decided she wanted to use what she had learned for her own personal gain. Desirous of more power than one person should have, she soon became out of control. The coven was forced to make a difficult decision and made arrangements to have her burned at the stake for the sake of the ones around them. When the deed was done, they went on with their lives. It seems that was not the end of her, though. Her ghost returned and began wreaking havoc upon the countryside, taking her revenge against the townspeople for having been betrayed by her sisters.

The women decided to bind her spirit to stop her once and for all, to keep their village safe."

Cassie set her fork aside, completely enthralled in the story. "How?"

Jessie tossed the cloth over her shoulder and thought for a moment. "I believe there was something about using a ritual to call her spirit and entrapping it in a box for all eternity."

"What happened then?"

"They lived happily ever after? It is a *story* told to children in elementary school around Halloween to get them in the spirit, after all." Jessie chuckled. "And it must be a good one since I managed to reel the archaeologist in hook, line, and sinker."

"Okay, I admit it! You got me!" Cassie relaxed and laughed at herself. "Sorry, I tend to get caught up in these things. Growing up in Salem, I have a special place in my heart for witchcraft lore, and it suckers me in every time!"

"Don't apologize!" Jessie patted her hand. "Tis the season, after all, but if you are interested in more about the history of the area, there is a small museum in town where you could find more information."

"Great! I will make it a priority to check it out!"

An hour later, Cassie sat parked in front of the security trailer at the dig site. The sun had just come up and an eerie silence, along with an odd feeling of uneasiness, filled the air. The security guard should have come outside as soon as she arrived, but no one had appeared. Blowing the horn a few times, she waited another ten minutes before going over and banging on the door.

"HELLO! IS ANYONE IN THERE?"

Receiving no response, Cassie tried the latch, only to find it unlocked. Pushing it open, she was surprised to find the lights and a small tv on, but no one anywhere in sight. Two full cups of coffee rested on the counter. Picking one up to find it ice cold, her gut screamed something was off.

"What the hell?" she muttered and walked out and then into the pitched tent. A strange thick fog rolled in from under the canvas, low to the ground, and from the direction of the circle of remains. Grabbing a flashlight from the table, she went out the back end, astonished to see that the mist appeared to be originating from the center and clinging to the curves of the circle as if there were a barrier of some sort keeping it in place.

"Ok, that's creepy!" Flicking on the light, she shined it around and called out for the guards once more, only to be met with silence. Moving the beam around, she walked out into the center of the circle, tripping over something rather large, causing her to fall to her hands and knees, dropping her light.

Unable to see because of the denseness of the fog, she felt around on the ground for the flashlight. "There you are!" she mumbled as her fingers closed around the small handle. Angling it to see what she had taken the tumble over, she gasped in horror when her mind registered what lay before her. Pulse racing and numbness overtaking her, she developed a terrible cramp in the pit of her stomach as her breakfast threatened to come back up.

"Oh my God!" Cassie exclaimed, scrambling backward and away.

One of the security guards from the day before was lying sprawled on his back, his eyes fixed open with an expression of horror on his face. His skin was blackened as if he had been burned to a crisp. The acrid smell of scorched flesh assaulted her senses as she moved, falling and stumbling, trying to get to her feet in an attempt to escape the gruesome scene. Pulling her phone out of her pocket, she finally made it to the tent and managed to dial, her hands trembling uncontrollably.

"Cassie? Why are you calling so early?" Thomas answered and asked, sleepily, on the third ring. "Is everything alright?"

"Thomas! He's dead!"

"What?" he demanded, suddenly wide awake. "Who's dead? What are you talking about? Where are you?"

"The security guard," her voice shaky, "I came to the site early and he's out there—dead."

"What happened to him?"

"I don—I don't know!" she stuttered. "He's lying in the middle of the excavation site."

"Are you there alone?"

"Ye—yes!"

"Listen to me! I don't know what's going on, but you need to get somewhere safe. Can you get inside the trailer?"

"Yeah! I think so!"

"Good! Go there now and lock the door! There's a bolt on the inside. Do it while I have you on the phone, so I know you're safe."

She nodded to herself and broke into a panicked sprint for the unit. Once inside, she secured the door, dropped to the floor, and blew out a hard breath. "I'm in!"

"Good! Don't move! I'm on my way!"

The local authorities arrived only moments before Thomas did. Cassie had managed to compose herself somewhat by then and met them at the door, leading them to the location of the body. The strange fog had dissipated, making the man hard to miss. Still unnerved, she wrapped her arms around herself and stepped out of the way to allow them room to conduct their investigation.

"Cassie! Are you alright?" She turned when she heard Thomas shout from his truck.

He hurried over and took her into a soothing embrace.

"I am, just a little shaken up," she replied, grateful to have him there with his arms around her. He had always been the one person who knew exactly how to comfort her. "I wasn't expecting to see a 'fresh' set of remains out here. Bones I can handle—flesh and blood—not so much."

"It's alright! I'm here now!" He took off his jacket and wrapped it around her shoulders. Turning his head, he grimaced, when he caught the strong odor of sulfur wafting on the air. "What the hell is that?" he asked. Letting go of her, he walked over to see the body for himself. "What on Earth happened to him?"

"Looks like he was fried crispy," smarted one of the officers, who was crouched down hovering over the victim, a handkerchief pressed to his face to cover the stench. "Did you know him?"

"Yes!" Thomas acknowledged. "He is a fill-in night security guard by the name of Ralph Knotts. He's only worked for me a couple of days. I always keep someone out here around the clock to keep the teenagers and occult fanatics out."

"Are there any electrical lines running through here?" the policeman asked.

"No!" Thomas pulled up the collar of his shirt and over his nose to breathe through. "We run everything off batteries and generators. Contractors aren't allowed to do any type of work like that on the property until we have given the 'all clear'." He regarded the officer. "You don't think he was electrocuted, do you?"

"I don't know what happened to him—not even sure I WANT to know," the man stood, "and lucky for me, it's not my problem anymore."

"Not your problem?" asked Cassie warily, hanging back a bit from the horrific scene. "What do you mean? Isn't finding out what happened to him part of your job?"

"Not anymore!" The man dipped his head towards the road. "It's HIS!"

Cassie and Thomas turned to see a tall, dark-haired man, wearing sunglasses and a casual suit, instructing the other men to rope off a large section of the area. Taking a hard look around and tightening his jaw, he affixed a badge to the front of this belt before striding over to join them. She couldn't put her finger on it, but something seemed oddly familiar about him, though she was sure she had never met the man before in her life.

"Who called this in?" he demanded as he approached.

Cassie raised her hand. "That would be me. I'm Dr. Cassie Summers, the on-site archaeologist."

"And I'm Dr. Thomas Armstrong, the one in charge of this excavation. Who are you?"

"I am Agent Richard Parker with the SB," he replied, his attention now focused on the body.

"The SB?" Thomas did not seem pleased. "I wasn't aware this sleepy little town had any SB agents close by, and furthermore, why would you be involved? Isn't this something the local authorities should be handling?"

"Your discovery has been of some interest recently, and I just happened to be in town on other business. I was packed up and ready to leave when I received the call."

"The 'SB'?" whispered a confused Cassie.

"Special Branch," the newcomer clarified before Thomas had the chance to answer. "We are a unit that reports directly to MI5 on matters of national security and intelligence."

"Why the hell is the SB interested in a centuries-old cemetery?" questioned Thomas. "Surely, you don't believe a yard full of bones is going to rise up and take down the government!"

"We just like to be aware of what's going on in our backyard," replied Agent Parker, his expression a bit smug, "and it's no longer just an 'old cemetery'," his eyes swept the area, "it's now the scene of a rather questionable death." Screwing up his face, he moved closer and raised the back of his hand to his nose when the smell of burnt flesh overwhelmed him.

"Hardly questionable!" Thomas, who was normally reserved, was unusually flustered by the man's presence. "There was a terrible storm here late yesterday. If I had to venture a guess, I would say he was probably struck by lightning."

The agent bent down. "Only he's not wet. If he was struck in the storm, his hair and clothes would have been soaked by the rain. Besides, that storm was yesterday evening, and I am not certain this man has been lying here that long."

"How can you be sure?"

"I can't until an autopsy is performed, but years of experience, along with my gut, tells me this was not caused by Mother Nature."

"Where's the other one?" Cassie asked suddenly, looking around. "There were two security guards here when we left yesterday, and there were two cups of coffee in the trailer."

"Two? You are certain?" the agent asked, straightening up.

"Yes, she's right!" Thomas turned. "I always pay an extra to be on duty overnight."

"Search the area! There may be another body out here!" shouted Agent Parker to the local authorities. "A couple of you go check the woods over there."

Cassie concentrated on the scene, trying to determine if anything was different from the day before. It was then she noticed one of the tarps that had previously been secured was now curled on one end. Cautiously, making her way over, she carefully lifted the corner just enough to see a trouser-covered leg and shoe poking out. Pulling it off, she discovered the second man in the last place she would have ever expected.

The initial set of remains, which had been dug out by the excavator had been placed in a temporary grave where the soil had been hollowed out, about a foot in depth—and the man was lying face down atop the first of the thirteen sets of remains that had been discovered. The most disturbing part was that the bones from the fingers were imbedded in his cheeks as if he had been taken into a lover's kiss, only *his* fingers were buried in the soil above the skull as if he had frantically tried to free himself.

"He's over here!" she called out, unable to tear her eyes away from the unnaturally ghoulish scene.

Thomas and Agent Parker reached her at the same time, both drawing back as they peered over the edge.

"I think it is safe to assume this one wasn't killed by lightning!" she remarked dryly.

"Do you have cameras on site?"

"Yes!" Thomas nodded slowly; his face clearly disturbed as he pointed with his thumb over his shoulder. "I'll go pull them up and see if they caught anything."

Agent Parker ordered one of the officers to accompany him to the trailer, before turning back to Cassie and donning a pair of latex gloves he had produced from his coat pocket. "What is your business here, Miss Summers?"

"*Dr.* Summers," she corrected, her attention still focused on the corpse as she replied matter-of-factly. "I told you before, I am an archaeologist. Thomas and I are old friends and colleagues. He wanted a second opinion on what he had discovered here, and I answered his call." Resting on her hands and knees, she craned her head to one side when something unusual caught her interest. Pointing, she asked, "Do you see that? I think there is something wedged between the teeth of the skull and the man's lips."

Parker parroted her position and followed her gaze intently. "I believe you're right. I'm not sure what it is, but I do see *something*!" Reaching inside his coat pocket, he pulled out a ballpoint pen and used it to pry the item free, careful not to disturb the rest of the scene. "What is that?"

"Do you have another pair of those gloves?" Cassie was now completely engrossed in the mystery that lay before them. The fact this man had died only a short time earlier did not deter her in the least. After gloving up, she reached down and picked up the item for a closer inspection. "It's a rune stone."

"A rune stone? What exactly is that and what is it used for?"

"Rune stones have been used since the fourth century for a variety of reasons, mostly by nomadic tribes during the Viking period. They were for anything from divination—to burials—to magical spells—and everything in between. Each symbol has a different meaning and is used in accordance with it. Some are as big as boulders and others are as small as a pair of bone dice."

"And that's unusual for this site?"

"Yeah, it is actually!" she rocked back on her haunches and held it up. "Each grave out here has had multiple ones in it, only…" she glanced down into the pit, then over her shoulder.

"Only what?"

"This skeleton is not in the place it was originally found. It was the first one to be discovered and was dug up accidentally by the construction company. All the stones found with it are bagged and tagged, locked up tight in the safe in the security trailer."

"What are you saying?"

Cassie flipped it over in her palm. "There is no way this stone was here before this man died. Thomas is a stickler for combing over sites, and he simply would not have missed something as important as this."

"You're that certain of his diligence?"

Cassie nodded. "One hundred percent! It was NOT there."

Parker took the rune from her hand. "What is the symbol specifically?"

Cassie sighed. "That is Algiz, the stone of protection."

"Well, it didn't seem to protect this guy," he pointed out.

"No, it certainly didn't," she looked around, "but it makes you wonder what needs protecting so badly out here."

Several hours later, after a lengthy round of questioning, the perimeter was still crawling with law enforcement and forensic teams. Cassie and Thomas propped themselves against the wall, out of the way, while Agent Parker and two others poured over the video, only to have it show nothing. Both deaths had occurred in areas where the cameras were not aimed. However, what sounded to be their final screams of death had been picked up by the surveillance video at around 3 a.m.

"Damn!" Parker leaned back in the chair and stroked his chin. After dismissing the other two men, he swiveled to face Cassie and Thomas. "Do either of you have any idea as to what might have happened out here last night? I'm extremely interested to hear the thoughts of the two people who last saw them alive."

Cassie and Thomas exchanged confounding glances before looking back to the agent, both at a loss for words.

"I am going to have to ask each of you where you were from the time you left here yesterday until this morning."

"Thomas and I went to dinner and back to the inn where I'm staying afterward," replied Cassie.

"You spent the night together?"

"No, we did not," Thomas clarified. "I took Cassie home, and we had a nightcap in the library before I went back to my place and straight to bed. I was fast asleep when she called this morning to tell me she had found the guard."

"Do you have any witnesses who can corroborate?"

"Do I need one?" snapped Thomas. "Are you implying we are suspects? You haven't even determined how they died! This may not even be a crime."

"SB procedure dictates that all unexplained deaths are treated as crimes, and everyone is a suspect until they are not. This will be handled as such until the autopsies prove otherwise," he replied nonchalantly.

"It is standard practice. So, I am to assume from your statement you have no alibi?"

"No, but I am certain you can ping my cell phone. That is the sort of work you do, is it not?" countered Thomas.

"It is, and I will," turning his attention to Cassie, "and you, Dr. Summers?"

"I went to bed after Thomas left. I couldn't sleep, so I got up and had breakfast with the innkeeper. That was well before dawn. Her name is Jessie, and I'm sure she will be happy to verify everything I have told you."

"Anything else?" asked Thomas. "We do have a site to excavate, and we would like to get back to it."

"Not today, you won't. This area is officially shut down until further notice."

"For how long?" Thomas's jaw tightened. "We are doing important work here. What about the priceless artifacts that could just be sitting out there unguarded? What if they are stolen and lost to history forever?"

"What about the men who died?" the agent fired back. "Don't you believe their families deserve to know what happened to them? To get answers about how and why their loved ones died?"

"Of course!" Thomas exhaled sharply, pausing to compose himself. "Forgive me," he said through gritted teeth, "it's been a difficult morning. We believe we are on the verge of a historically significant find, and I am more than a little anxious to get to it."

"I can have officers posted around the clock to secure the area, but until we figure out what happened to those men, it will remain closed."

He began to protest, but Cassie took him by the arm. "Thomas, it's okay!" She managed a half-smile. "Whatever is out there has been out here this long—a few more days isn't going to make that much difference."

"You know as well as I do what we are potentially sitting on here," he whispered.

"And it isn't going anywhere," she reassured. "Agent Parker is right. Let him figure out what happened so we don't have anything hanging over us when we finally do piece this mystery together."

"Of course, you're right!" Thomas calmed down and his anger dissipated. "Agent, is it alright if I get some of my papers and maps out of the main tent so I will have something to keep me occupied while you are conducting your investigation?"

Parker thought for a moment and nodded. "As long as one of the officers accompanies you, and everything is witnessed and recorded."

"Thank you!" Turning to Cassie, he said, "Let me grab what I need, and I'll see you safely back to the inn."

Once they were alone, Cassie and the agent quietly studied each other.

It was Parker who broke the awkward silence. "You're American?"

Cassie scoffed. "Your powers of observation are astounding, Agent Parker.".

The corners of his lips twitched up. "While it is true, they will let anyone join the SB these days, you must have a few special skills for them to keep you around on a more permanent basis." Drumming his fingers on the desk, he asked, "Will you be staying on?"

"I will. I already promised Thomas my help and that has not changed."

"Are the two of you very close?"

Cassie shifted on her feet uncomfortably. "We used to be when I was in college. He was one of my professors and went on to become a good friend. I haven't seen much of him since then, but we've stayed in touch."

"You were remarkably calm out there, given you had just discovered not one, but two, dead bodies. Did that not upset you?"

"It most certainly did, Agent. You should have seen me before everyone else got here. 'Calm' was not the word I would have used to describe my initial reaction from tripping over a fresh corpse. 'Mortified', 'shocked', 'frightened beyond belief', yes— 'calm', no! I am used to the dead, just not them being so…" a visible shiver shook her, "'juicy'."

Agent Parker cocked his head. "No, I don't suppose you are accustomed to that. Why were you out here so early all by yourself anyway?"

Cassie shrugged. "Sometimes it's easier for me to put pieces together when no one else is around. Besides, I enjoy the solitude of working alone before anyone else gets in. Things often become clearer in the peace and quiet of the early morning dawn." The truth was, she was hoping to get her hands on some of the relics from the site to help her figure out exactly what they had stumbled on. The only caveat with her gift was that she needed to take the objects in hand, without gloves, and concentrate to get a vision, a mental safeguard granted by the universe that kept her from being overwhelmed by everything she touched. If she could manage some time alone with the stone pulled from the death scene, she might be able to pick up on the victim's final moments. "I don't suppose we could get back that rune we found on the dead man?"

Parker scrubbed his jawline. "It will be returned eventually after we solve the crime, if there was one, but that could take some time."

"There is no way I could borrow it for the night? Maybe? I promise I will give it back tomorrow?" She winced when she realized how ludicrous the request sounded aloud.

Agent Parker was suddenly intrigued. "Why do you need it?"

"It may be important to our find, but I would need some time alone—to study it a little closer," she lied. "I might even be able to figure out why it was on the guard's body."

"That's not going to happen," he stated resolutely, pulling a notebook from his coat pocket. "Where are you staying?"

"'The Witch's Globe'. It is about three miles up the road."

"I'm familiar with the place. I will be in touch, Dr. Summers." Pulling a card from his pocket, he handed it to her. "If anything comes to mind that might be useful, please don't hesitate to give me a call."

"How are you doing?" asked Thomas as they stood outside the inn. "I know this wasn't the morning we had hoped for."

"I could have done without all the extra excitement," she replied, still a bit unsteady. He reached across and grasped her by the hand comfortingly.

"I need to pay a visit to the property owner in town, explain what's happened, and let the workers know what's going on, but it can all wait if you want me to stay. I want to make certain you are alright. Today has been a bit overwhelming, to say the least."

"Don't worry about me. You have your hands full." Frowning, she asked the question aloud, "What *do* you think happened out there?"

Thomas shook his head. "Honestly, Cassie, I don't know what to think. I have never seen anything like this before in all my days. I will be very interested in hearing what the autopsies reveal. I know I didn't do it, and you didn't do it, so we don't have anything to worry about from the authorities. They will get it sorted out soon enough, I have no doubt." Tightening his hold, "Are you sure you don't want me to stay?"

"No, you have enough to deal with. We can touch base later."

"Call me if you need me, or if you just want to talk. I can be here in no time." He leaned across and tenderly kissed her. "Have I told you how happy I am you're here?"

"It never hurts to hear it said again."

She watched him get back in his truck, waving as he drove off. Jessie met her at the door, pulling her into an unexpected embrace. "Cassie! Thank goodness! I heard what happened, and I've been worried to death about you. Are you alright?"

"Yeah, I'm fine. It just hasn't been the best of days. How did you find out?"

"It's a small town and word gets around, especially when someone dies. Neither one of the men lived here, but we feel the loss just the same." Jessie put her arm around her shoulders and walked her into the kitchen. "I made chocolate chip cookies in case you wanted to talk. I thought you might need some comfort food after a day like today."

"Jessie, you are an angel!" Cassie took a bite of one and sighed, grateful for the treat and the company as she sank down in a chair. "It was awful! I have never seen anything like it before."

"What exactly happened to them?" Jessie pulled out the chair and sat down across from her.

"I wish I knew. It was just—so weird. One looked and smelled like he had been burned and the other— the expression on his face was one of pure horror. I don't know what to think." Her face contorted and a noticeable shiver overtook her body. "I know I will never forget that smell for as long as I live."

"Well, I know what I think," said Jessie empathetically. "I think you and I are going to spend tonight eating the rest of these cookies, drinking whisky, watching crappy television, and putting this shitty day behind us."

Cassie smiled, Jessie having quickly become her new favorite person. "I think I like the way you think."

Jessie had her own private three-bedroom house separate from the rest of the inn, discreetly connected by a long, ivy-covered walkway. Cassie was surprised to see how spacious and modern it was compared to the richly colored and cozy inn adorned with antiques and period pieces.

"Your place is gorgeous and nothing like I expected!" she marveled.

"Oh, thank you!" replied Jessie, filling the already full coffee table with even more snacks. "I love running the inn, but we girls need to have our own space to escape to. I'm sure you know what I mean!"

"This is much better than mine. You don't have to fold your bed into the wall to get into your kitchen."

Jessie laughed and poured two glasses of whisky, inviting her to sit. "That's right. You did say you spent a great deal of time away from home."

"All the time actually. Usually, on rare occasions when I'm not working, I fly to the east coast to visit my mom. My dad passed away a while back and I like to keep check on her."

"That's the 'daughterly' thing to do. I'm sure your mother appreciates it."

"By the way, thank you for this. I haven't sat down and watched tv with someone else since— well, I guess since college now that I think about it." Memories of her late nights with Bethany flooded her mind.

"Oh sweetie, everyone needs a girlfriend for nights like this." Jessie handed her a blanket and spread one across her own lap. "You must have someone you're close with back home."

"I used to." She accepted the bowl of popcorn Jessie passed to her and popped a piece in her mouth. "My roommate Bethany and I were as close as sisters, but she passed away in a car accident a few weeks before our graduation from college."

"That's terrible. I'm so sorry that happened."

"Yeah, me too. I still miss her every day." Each word and every detail from when Thomas told her the news was fresh in her mind. Seeing him had brought it all back.

"How did you end up here of all places?" Jessie settled in and sipped from her glass.

"Bethany and I became close with Thomas—the one in charge of this dig—when he taught at our college. He was new to the area and wasn't much older than we were. The three of us ended up becoming the best of friends. When I got the call he needed help, I couldn't say 'no'. He was there to pick up the pieces when I fell apart, and I don't think I would have made it through without his shoulder to lean on when she died."

"Sounds like the two of you became more than 'close'."

"We did—we were—for a little while. He was exactly what I needed at the time, but he was called back to London on family business. We were never the same after that—long-distance relationships and all."

Jessie took a handful of popcorn. "And now?"

"I am not sure where we stand in that regard. I have to admit, I was pleasantly surprised when he kissed me last night. It was—nice."

"Nice?" Jessie wrinkled her nose and stuck out her tongue. "I am not sure 'nice' is what keeps a girl warm at night."

"It beats having to be 'nice' to yourself, and I have had to do that way too much lately!" muttered Cassie sarcastically. The two burst into laughter.

"What about you? Any special person in your life being 'nice' to you?"

"There might be one or two I see when the urge hits," she replied wistfully, "but none on a regular basis. I prefer to keep my options open, so I have the freedom to do as I please with whomever I choose and whenever I like."

Cassie lifted her glass in a toast. "There's a lot to be said for freedom!"

"Absolutely!" Jessie raised her own and clinked. "Cheers!"

The women stayed up until the early hours of the morning, watching movies, drinking, and laughing. Comfortably numb from the alcohol and the shock from the day's events now sufficiently dulled in her mind, Cassie stumbled back to her room and noticed she had missed two calls and a text from Thomas. Collapsing face-first across the bed, she fell asleep without giving him a second thought. Late the next morning, she returned his call before making her way downstairs in search of caffeine, sugar, and aspirin for her hangover headache.

Cassie stopped in the doorway and rubbed her eyes with her palm, her mind taking a minute to register what she was seeing.

"Agent Parker?"

"Ah, Dr. Summers, good morning," he replied looking up from the folded newspaper he was reading.

"What are you doing here?"

"Well, he's staying with us," replied Jessie as she placed a full plate of food and a cup of coffee at one of the seats, "and good morning! I hope you managed to get some sleep last night."

"Good morning, and yes, I did. Thank you for the company. I needed that!"

Jessie winked and handed her a bottle of aspirin, which she immediately made use of. Cassie turned to the new arrival, washing the pills down with her coffee. "Since when are you staying here?"

Parker took a sip from his cup. "Since the place I was staying at had other guests who had booked the house beginning today. When I stopped by to verify your whereabouts at the time of the crime, which Miss Reed kindly corroborated with her well-placed security cameras, she mentioned she had an open room. It seems I will be here for a while, so I decided to take her up on it."

Cassie took the seat next to him. "Have you found out anything more?"

"Not yet. I'm waiting on the autopsy reports—which I hope will be in later today. Miss Reed has also been kind enough to lend me the use of her office during my visit so I can stay on top of the findings."

"Is that an actual newspaper?" she asked, wondering how old this guy was. "I didn't know they still made those things."

"Well, we must have something to wrap our fish and chips in," he retorted, not missing a beat.

"It's hot off the press." Jessie chuckled. "Our newspaper only prints once a week because there's not enough news to run it every day. I get them delivered because the guests like to see what's happening in and around town."

"Count yourself lucky. There are worse places to live," remarked Cassie as she picked up her fork.

"I suppose California has more than enough news to justify printing each day."

"Actually, we have mostly moved into the twenty-first century. Online news kills fewer trees and is better for the ecosystem. We are all about saving the environment in Cali." Cassie stopped her fork midway to her mouth. "Have you been checking up on me, Agent Parker?"

"I have, but I assure you, it's all routine. I had background checks done on everyone from the dig. It was all done online. Fewer pages to print to save the trees, if it makes you feel any better."

"Well, sorry to disappoint you, but I have nothing to hide." She took a bite of her food. "The bones I dig up have livelier lives than I do." Pausing, she grimaced when she realized that was actually the truth. Maybe she could use a little more excitement in her life—the good kind anyway.

"What are your plans for the day, Cassie?" asked Jessie.

"Thomas and I are grabbing lunch and then going to do some research since we can't work."

"You two spend a great deal of time together, don't you?" inquired Parker.

Cassie bobbed her head from side to side. "The nature of the business, I suppose."

"What's it like being an archaeologist?" he asked. "Do you have a hat and a bullwhip like that Indiana

Jones fellow? Have you found any priceless cursed statues or Holy Grails?"

Cassie laughed into her napkin. "No, but he may have played a small part in my decision to become one. I don't mind saying, I thought I would be finding way more in gold treasure than I have."

"I don't know, you've done pretty well in the field given the stack of accolades attached to your name."

"I don't care about those," she said quietly and sipped her coffee. "They usually hand them out at those fancy galas I avoid like the plague. It's more about the thrill of the hunt for me. Sure, the hours are long, the work is dirty, and running water is in short supply, but nothing compares to the thrill of holding something in your hands that hasn't seen the light of day for centuries. Standing in a museum, watching a child's eyes light up with wonder when they see something like that for the very first time and learning the story behind it—that's where the real treasure is."

"It sounds like you love your work."

"I honestly do, and I wouldn't trade it for anything. I don't know many folks who can say that."

"Where are you doing your research?" Jessie refilled their cups.

"I'm not sure. Thomas said he had somewhere special he wanted to take me that might shed some light on the excavation."

"What is out there?" probed Parker curiously.

"Excuse me?"

"What is your friend so interested in digging up? He seems very anxious to get back to it."

"It's an unusual burial site and it may have a great deal of historical significance."

"In what way?"

Cassie hesitated but decided being up front, given the circumstances, would be the best for all concerned. "Given the rune stones and the placements of the bodies, we think it may be a witch cemetery from the sixteenth century."

"And there is something unusual about that in itself?" Parker gave her his full attention, his interest sufficiently piqued.

"While we can't be certain of anything until we excavate the entire site, the carbon dating that was conducted indicates it goes back further than expected, most likely at a time when documented witch-hunters would have not yet arrived in this area. Given the rune stones and the layout, it suggests more of a ceremonial burial by *other* witches, something those of us in the field have never seen the likes of before."

Jessie rested her forearms on the counter and leaned down. "Wait! Wouldn't that have been near impossible to pull off in a small area like this during a time when even suspected witches were being burned at the stake for no apparent reason?"

"Exactly!" replied Cassie, impressed by her logic. "Which is why it is so puzzling. Can you imagine burying thirteen bodies, all in peculiar positions with rune stones, and no one taking notice or being concerned? And to do it on a spot where someone had been burned at the stake? That would have been hard to miss."

"Wait!" Parker held up his hand. "Burned at the stake? What makes you think that?"

"Pieces of charred wood indicate a large spot of the ground, roughly the size of a pyre that would have been used for that reason, was scorched at around the same time."

"What would have been the purpose of that?"

"That's what we intend to find out—as soon as you finish your job, that is, Agent Parker, so we can get back to ours."

Cassie glanced down at her watch and stood. "If you will excuse me, I need to get ready. Thomas will be here to pick me up soon."

When she reached the doorway, Parker called out, "Dr. Summers, did it ever occur to you that some things might be best left undisturbed?"

"No!" She paused and pondered the rest of her answer. "We can only make our future a better place if we learn from our past mistakes, and we can't learn from our past mistakes if we don't know our history. The things I dig up are serving no purpose in the ground, but there is good reason to remove them for study." She started towards the stairs.

"I wouldn't be so sure about that, Dr. Summers!" he called out.

5

CHAPTER FIVE

Thomas picked her up an hour later, and after a long, leisurely lunch, he drove her to a small house in the middle of town. Cassie was confused until she saw the sign reading 'North Elmham Historical Society' and underneath that, in extremely tiny letters, 'Home of the Witch Box'.

"A witch museum with a witch box?"

"Well, a museum with some occult items!" he clarified and turned off the engine. "They don't have much, but I thought it might be worth a look. Don't you want to know what we are up against and how we can protect ourselves?"

Cassie rolled her eyes. "You are taking Halloween a little too seriously this year."

"I am willing to admit I may be a little more inclined to superstition given what I have seen over the past few weeks." Thomas grinned. "A smart man understands when he is out of his element. It is always prudent to arm yourself with as much knowledge as possible. Besides, I know how much you love all things Halloween, and we do seem to have some time to kill. The least I can do to express my gratitude is to show you a good time while you are here." He nudged her with his shoulder. "Come on, don't pretend you aren't dying to go in there. I know you better than that!"

A broad smile spread across her face, and she opened the passenger door. "I'd be lying if I said I wasn't." Giddy as a schoolgirl, she laughed and slid out of her seat to race for the door. "The last one inside is a rotten egg!"

The museum was extremely small in comparison to most, only encompassing three downstairs rooms of a partially renovated house, but it was filled with artifacts, all procured from the local area.

No one else was visiting that day, and Ilene, their 'Historical Society Hostess', left them to roam at their leisure. "Feel free to ask if you have any questions," she called out, not bothering to look up as she licked the end of her finger and turned the page of her romance novel with the strong, muscular Scotsman adorning the front cover.

"Not a big tourist attraction, I see," muttered Cassie.

"I can honestly say I don't think Ilene minds," he whispered back.

The two held hands, taking their time and wandering through while studying the different artifacts. Finally, they located the extremely small 'witchcraft' section. It contained a few items, mostly iron needles, pieces of chain, and the printed replication of a seventeenth-century checklist on parchment paper aptly named, 'Is Your Neighbor a Witch?'. Thomas stepped closer to the publication, pulling out his glasses for a better look. Cassie, however, found herself drawn to a peculiar-looking chest with rune symbols carved inside the lid locked up in a glass case with a sign identifying it as 'The Witch Box'.

"Ilene, what do you know about this?" she called over her shoulder.

The older woman laid her book aside and stood up. "Oh, that was discovered near the ruins of an old church dating back to the late 1500s. The museum fellow who found it, for some reason, believed it was used to bind an evil spirit. If you look closely, you will see it was sealed with wax before it was buried in hallowed ground."

"Um!" Cassie wagged her finger. "Did anybody pay any attention to the little fact that the seal is broken?"

Ilene shrugged. "That's how it was discovered."

Cassie looked to Thomas who had a mischievous smirk on his face as she asked, "You folks haven't had any vengeful witches roaming the land exacting revenge lately, have you?"

"Hardly! Personally, I think I would be more concerned about the *living* witches." A peculiar look suddenly crossed her face. "Of course, then again, there are those two dead bodies they found over where they have been digging around for another unnecessary shopping center, so maybe there is something to it after all."

"Yeah, that would be us," Cassie confessed with a wince. "Just two archaeologists out here doing our thing."

Ilene rested one hand on her hip and peered over the rim of her glasses. "I don't suppose it ever occurred to you to let the dead rest in peace?"

"Why does everyone keep asking me that?" muttered Cassie under her breath.

"I assure you," Thomas interjected, "we are doing it with the most honorable of intentions and are using due diligence to preserve the historical aspects of the area."

"Hmph! Tell that to the two dead men," she mumbled, adjusting her glasses and going back to reading her book. "They started restoring the church where that artifact was discovered a few years ago but ran out of funding before they could complete it. What's left of it is out on the edge of town if you want to see it for yourself. It's become a popular destination for wedding photos, of all things. If you do visit though, do try not to ruin that spot like you did the other by digging up matters better left buried!"

"Maybe we should go," Cassie mouthed to Thomas.

Thomas nodded and escorted her outside, calling 'thank you' over his shoulder.

Resting his hands on the steering wheel back inside the truck, he asked, "Well, what do you say? Are you up for exploring the original resting place of 'The Witch Box'?"

"Heck yeah! Let's go!"

The crumbling church ruins were nothing short of astounding. Though the roof no longer existed, and only a few partial walls still stood, the ancient stones emitted a numinous enchantment. The couple carefully made their way inside to find what was left of an early altar near the front. Unable to resist, Cassie rested her hand flat against the stone, closed her eyes, and concentrated. A vision came together in her mind of the church when it was newly constructed and bursting at the seams with parishioners joyfully basking in the presence of the Lord. A warmth filled her from within and a smile emerged as she was reminded of what a wonderful gift her ability truly was.

"You seem very wistful and at peace," remarked Thomas, joining her, "especially given all you witnessed yesterday."

"I will admit, yesterday was pretty bad, but…" she moved her hand and the picture faded, "I can't soak up enough of the energy of these old places, especially where people were once so happy. It helps to make up for the shitty days."

"How do you know they were happy?" he asked, his hands in his pockets as he lightly brushed against her shoulder with his.

Her eyes swept over the ruins. "I just know," she replied and turned to face him. "I can certainly see why brides are drawn to this place. The sense of love ingrained into these stones and walls is palatable and there was certainly an enormous amount of it here at one time. Human beings are sensitive to things like that, whether they know it or not."

"That's one of the many things I always loved about Cassie Summers—her knack for finding serenity even in the darkest of storms."

"You know better than anyone that there was a certain period in my life when that wasn't possible for me, but over the years, I have slowly found my way back to it."

"I am sure Bethany would be pleased to hear it. She loved you very much and would have despised seeing you as lost as you were after her death."

Taking him by the hand, she led him outside where they could still make out the lines of the outer wall surrounding the church, enclosing the cemetery. A few weathered headstones with the writing long worn smooth dotted the area around the structure.

"Where do you think they found it?" he asked, stopping to brush the leaves off the top of one of the gravestones.

"What? The box?" Cassie wandered around, bending over to read epitaphs wherever a few letters still existed. "Good question. It looks like it's been a while since anyone dug here, but if I had to venture a guess," she commented as some inner intuition guided her over to a particular spot. Just as she reached it, a chill rushed down her spine. "I would say it was right about here."

"Why there?" he questioned, folding his arms with intense curiosity.

"Not too close, but still inside the walls, and on hallowed ground, not to mention," she shielded her eyes with her hand and looked towards the church as if gauging the distance, "on a far corner that is easy to access under the cover of darkness," a grin spread across her face and she pointed down, "and—oh yeah, this tiny metal marker that says an unusual box was discovered right here!"

Thomas's demeanor relaxed and he laughed, ambling over to join her. "Something tells me the brilliant Dr. Summers, as always, is correct." They both dropped to their knees and began to clear off the freshly cut grass. Before they could finish, the lightly overcast sky darkened, and the heavens opened.

"It seems the rain has it in for us." Thomas sighed, standing and helping her to her feet. They rushed back to his truck, and once again, found themselves soaked to the bone. "I did, however, come prepared this time!" Grabbing a towel from the backseat, he used the corner to gently blot the wetness from her face.

"God, you are even more beautiful than you were in college," he whispered, their eyes finding each other. Tenderly, he brushed a strand of loose hair away from her cheek. "My place isn't far from here. What do you say we spend the rest of this gloomy afternoon there?"

"I think that sounds perfect."

Thomas made a delicious pasta carbonara that evening as he had done so many times for her and Bethany all those years ago. They reminisced about their old friend and the wonderful times they had together. After finishing off a bottle of wine, they slowly made their way from the kitchen to his bedroom. Pieces of clothing were peeled away as they moved, and they reached his bed more than halfway undressed. More than ready to take it to the next level, the couple became distracted by the incessant, repeated ringing of his phone.

"Oh, for God's sake!" Thomas grumbled, fumbling on the nightstand to find the offending item and shut it off. When he saw who it was, he cursed under his breath. "I need to take this."

Cassie rolled on her side and used her fingertips to trace over the three small Celtic tattoos on his shoulder, listening to the conversation. It was an urgent call from the property owner demanding Thomas come to his office at once. He hit the end button and threw the phone across the room out of frustration.

Turning to face her, he pressed his forehead to hers and groaned before apologizing profusely. "I'm afraid I have to go. If I could avoid this, I would, but this client has a great deal of clout in the field. One damaging word from him could ruin me and I cannot afford to lose the business." He swung his legs over the side. "I'm sorry! I wanted nothing more than to spend the rest of this day here in this bed making love to you."

"I know the feeling," she said with an exasperated sigh, resting her hand on his back. "But I do understand."

He shifted and kissed her once more, growling as he reached for his shirt. "I promise, I will make this up to you as soon as humanly possible."

Cassie reclined back and pulled the sheet to her breast. "And I will hold you to it!"

6

CHAPTER SIX

Thomas reluctantly drove her back to the inn and
escorted her to the door, promising to check in later.
He left her hanging with a long, sensual kiss. Sighing,
she brushed her fingers across her lips before going
inside. She was still smiling when she found Agent
Parker sitting in a chair by the fireplace in the library.

"Ah, Dr. Summers, your timing is impeccable."

"Just call me 'Cassie' please, Agent Parker," she said
with a dismissive wave of a hand.

"Cassie, it is! And please, just call me Parker," he
reciprocated. His tone was a great deal less formal,
friendly even. "I have the autopsy results if you're
interested."

"I am, I mean if I am allowed to see them!" she
replied, crossing the room.

"I think I can make an exception for you." Parker shook the file in his hand. "According to this, the first man was burned, his internal organs seemingly boiled from the inside out." He handed her the report. "The fire began at the base of his feet and moved upward, yet there were no signs of a blaze at the scene, and then there is the matter of his clothes remaining completely unscorched—not even so much as a cigarette burn hole."

"How is that possible?" She sank into the chair across from him.

"That is the question of the day. There were also no indications of lightning, electrocution, or anything else along those lines. The coroner is scratching his head, at a complete loss, even going so far as to suggest spontaneous internal combustion, of all things."

"What about the second man?" she asked as she skimmed the page.

"Asphyxiation, complete with bruising that indicated he had been choked to death. I think you might be interested in reading page four."

Cassie flipped through it until her eyes fell on a photo that sent a chill down her spine. The forensics team had bagged up the skeleton hands when collecting evidence and the marks on his necks lined up perfectly—a picture had been included with the finger bones to demonstrate.

"What the fuck?" she muttered, staring at the page. "Are you suggesting the second man was murdered by a four-hundred-year-old skeleton?"

Parker stood and reached for a decanter of whisky, pouring two glasses, and handing her one. "I am not sure what I am suggesting. I have been in this world for forty years and I have seen things in my job that would make a sane person check themselves into the nearest institution, begging to be medicated for life, but this—" he paused and retook his seat across from her, "this disturbs me more than I care to admit."

"Could someone have done this to them somewhere else and dumped their bodies at the dig site?" she asked and handed him back the file.

"You saw the same surveillance video and time stamp I did. There wouldn't have been enough time, and besides, we heard their screams right after they left for their rounds. They most certainly died where they were discovered." He studied her closely as the next words came from his lips. "Why do I have a feeling there is something about that dig site you have not mentioned, like your own theory perhaps?"

"You think it matters?"

"I most certainly do. Look, I'm just trying to put the puzzle pieces together. Their families deserve some closure."

Cassie hesitated.

"Come on! You are the expert!" he encouraged. "Thirteen bodies, found with rune stones and laid out in a ritualistic manner—for what reason? Dr. Summers—Cassie! Two men are dead and there is something you are not saying! It is as plain as the nose on your face."

"I am convinced there is something historically important in the middle of that circle, but I am not sure what it is yet, or who else would even know about it."

"Do you think it's worth killing someone over?"

"I have no idea, but even I have to admit, the timing does seem a little suspect. There's also no way to know until I can get back to work."

"Well, you can't get back to work until I figure out what happened out there, so it seems we are at a stalemate. In the morning, I'm going to formally request the government shut the site down permanently."

"You can't do that!" she argued. "Do you know how important this could be?"

He leaned forward. "It's not worth taking a chance on someone else dying. I won't let it happen on my watch if there is some way to prevent it."

"You are assuming the two are connected, and you have no way of knowing that."

"I have no way of knowing there are not!" he countered. "In the meantime, I am not willing to risk it. I'm sorry!" He downed his drink and stood. "Good night, Cassie."

There was no way he would release the crime scene without finding out what happened and there was only one surefire way to make that happen sooner rather than later. Struggling with her conscience versus the thought of the find, she made an impetuous decision. When he reached the door, she lowered her head, scrunched up her face, and called out through gritted teeth, "Wait!"

He turned.

"What if there were a way to figure out what happened? If it can be determined their deaths had nothing to do with the actual dig site, or you discover it was a deliberate attempt to shut it down, would you be willing to open it back up?"

"Possibly!" His eyes narrowed in on her. "Cassie, if you are holding back information on a crime…"

"I'm not! But I may know of a way of getting some information useful to the case."

Parker pulled the pocket doors closed and went back over to her. "I'm listening."

Cassie dropped her face into her hands, struggling with the decision she had just made. "If I tell you something, I need your word it will never go any further than this room. It is something I have never told another soul—not even my parents—and it is a secret I vowed as a child to never reveal to anyone else."

Slowly nodding his head, he sounded as astounded to say it as she was to hear it. "I give you my word."

Sensing her reluctance, he patiently waited for her to speak.

"When I turned thirteen, a woman came to me in a dream claiming to be my deceased great-grandmother to give me a gift—the ability to hold a relic in my hands, focus in on it, and harvest a vision from it. She told me no one else would understand, so I would have to keep it hidden."

Parker's brow creased as he made a few connections. "The rune stone you wanted to borrow from the body, that's why you asked for it?"

"Yes, I can't control what comes through, but it has never let me down before. It has helped me sort out many mysteries that would have otherwise gone unsolved and furthered my field for the better. If you can give me access to that stone, I promise, I will share with you everything it reveals to me."

Parker remained quiet for a long moment considering her offer. "Alright, I am willing to take a chance. Honestly, I am at a complete loss, and, at this point, I am open to just about anything."

"You believe me?"

"Are you lying?"

Cassie shook her head. "No, I'm not!"

"And I don't believe you are, either. In truth, my mind is a little more open to such things than I am willing to admit to my colleagues." He glanced towards the door. "The stone is in evidence at the local police station, but it is being picked up by a courier and taken back to our office in London first thing in the morning. If we do this, we will need to do it tonight."

Cassie was on her feet immediately. "Let's go! I'm ready!"

"Alright, I'll get my keys."

"How well do you know your friend, Dr. Armstrong?" he asked as they drove into town.

"Pretty well," she replied, glancing through the passenger window and wincing, recalling exactly how 'well' she had been getting reacquainted with him just a few hours ago. Not wanting to get into personal details, she scratched the side of her nose and continued. "He was one of my professors in college and we became close friends. We've kept in contact over the years, and he asked for my help on this gig."

"He left his teaching job the same week you graduated from what I understand. Is that correct?"

"Yes, he had some family business that called him back to London and decided not to return. We lost a dear friend at about the same time, and it was a difficult period for both of us."

"That would be Bethany Giles?"

Cassie turned to face him. "Exactly how deeply have you been digging into my past?"

He opened his mouth to say more, but stopped, pausing to consider his answer. Obviously, he had hit a nerve. "Please understand, Cassie, I am just doing my job," he said gently. "Two men lost their lives out on that property, and I have never been one to take my responsibilities lightly. I take my work very seriously."

She closed her eyes. "I know, I'm sorry," her tone softened. "It's just that Bethany and I were like sisters and, even after all this time, I guess that is a wound that is still a little raw."

"I understand completely, and I hope you will forgive me for bringing it up. I am afraid my many years at this job have made me a little rough around the edges."

"How did you end up in the—Special Branch? Is that what it is called?"

"Yes! I spent some time serving in the British Armed Forces and it just seemed like the next logical move. It would have been a difficult transition into a regular job and the suburban life after that anyway, so I simply didn't."

"No marriage or kids?"

Parker cringed, then chuckled. "Only a bitter ex-wife, and I never really had much of a desire for children."

"Yeah, me neither. I've never settled down, and I don't see myself as the 'mothering' type."

"Probably for the best. Those pesky kids are always wanting expensive toys to play with, not the four-hundred-year-old bones and rune stones you already have lying around," he joked.

Cassie snorted. "Yeah, something like that!"

When they arrived at the station, no one questioned the order when Parker had everything brought into a private room so they could be alone. "Here it is." He pulled the evidence bag from the box.

Cassie stared at it warily before loosening the seal and dropping the relic into her palm. Closing her eyes, she wrapped her fingers around it, centered herself, and asked for a vision.

After a few tense moments, her eyes suddenly flew open wide, and she flung the stone across the table as if it had singed her skin. Scrubbing her palm against her jeans, her face drained of color as she stared down at it, her body now trembling.

"Cassie, what the hell did you see?" demanded Parker, her overall appearance greatly concerning to him.

"It can't be!" she mumbled. "It's not possible!"

He moved closer. "What isn't possible?"

"I saw it, but I can't explain it!" Her eyes lifted to meet his. "He was strangled by that skeleton."

"Come again?"

"That's what I saw. That pile of bones took form, rose from the grave, and dragged him back into the ground with her. That poor bastard tried to fight back but he didn't stand a chance. She was just too powerful. And the other man, I saw him, as well. His ankles were held in place by a different pair of bony hands to the point there was no escape. Then the flames appeared from the ground, starting at the soles of his feet, flaring up as if he were being burned at the stake. They both died horrifically and in a great deal of agony."

Parker covered his mouth with his hand. "What exactly are you trying to say?"

Cassie's face was filled with disbelief, but her words were clear, leaving no doubt. "Those men were killed—by witchcraft!"

They drove back to the inn in silence, Cassie needing more time to contemplate her vision. Once inside, Parker pulled her into the library once more, closed the doors, and planted her in a chair.

"Witchcraft?" he finally managed, leaning against the wall with his arms crossed. "That's what you saw? Are the deceased somehow taking their revenge for being disturbed?"

"I'm not sure what I picked up on! I mean, that's what I saw, but how could it possibly have been real? The dead don't just rise from the grave. It just doesn't happen."

Holding up one hand, he conceded with a nod. "Okay, let's play devil's advocate for a moment, and say, purely for the sake of argument, the supernatural WAS responsible. What information can we learn from your vision? Were the spirits angry because their bodies were moved? Are they trying to relay a message of warning, or do they just want everyone gone from the land itself?"

"It's not like that. It was more like they were in defense mode. I felt what they felt, and their only aim was to protect whatever is in the middle of that damned circle. It was why they were placed there to begin with—as guardians of some sort."

"Exactly what are they protecting?"

"That's just it! I don't know, but whatever it is, it's important to them!" Cassie was suddenly exhausted, her visions had never affected her so intensely, mentally and physically, before. "You don't believe me," she muttered.

Parker moved to stand directly in front of her. "I believe you have been through a great ordeal finding two fresh corpses at your worksite and I think your mind may be playing tricks on you."

"Normally, I would agree with that assessment, but it wasn't just what I saw with my eyes. I felt an energy stronger than anything I have ever felt before!"

"I think you need some rest," he said gently. "I doubt you've had much sleep over the past few days and perhaps you will see things in a different light come morning."

Too tired to argue, she merely responded, "Okay, whatever!"

Parker helped her to her feet and took her safely to her room where he helped her get settled for the night. Remaining and watching over her warily until she fell asleep, he turned off the lights and quietly closed the door on his way out.

Once he was in the hall, he took his phone out of his pocket and made a call. "We need to put an end to this NOW before things spiral completely out of control. We are running out of time!"

That night, Cassie's dreams were overrun with flashes of Bethany and Thomas and their time together. Soon, they were joined by thirteen witches, reaching out with their hands trying to pull Cassie into the middle of their circle, beckoning her to join their deadly coven. They even knew her name, calling out and claiming her as one of their own. She tried to fight through the abyss and force herself awake, but the women held her in place, refusing to relinquish their hold upon her. When she declined, they closed in around her and dragged her to a freshly built wood pyre, where she was bound with rope and set aflame.

Cassie woke with a scream, tangled in her sheets, feeling like she was on fire and drenched in sweat.

7

CHAPTER SEVEN

Cassie finally drifted back off before dawn but was awakened by the buzzing of her phone. Groggy and bothered by the noise, she lifted the covers and patted them down, scrambling to find it. Locating it at the foot of the bed, she managed to answer on the fourth ring.

"Thomas?"

"Get dressed, darling. I will be there to pick you up in twenty minutes and wear your dig clothes."

She sat straight up. "My dig clothes? What's going on?"

"Well, you are now speaking to the new owner of the excavation site, and I think it's time we got back to work. I will explain everything once I get there!"

Cassie tossed on her clothing and rushed downstairs. The house and the kitchen were unusually quiet, which she found oddly disturbing, though she didn't know why. Grabbing a still-warm baked scone from a covered dish, she wolfed it down and chased it with a glass of juice. Hearing the beep of a horn, she grabbed her bag and rushed outside.

"Good morning, sweetheart!" Thomas leaned over and took his time kissing her enthusiastically. "I am sorry I rushed off last night, but I think you will forgive me when I explain why."

"I am anxious to hear what happened," she said, fastening her seat belt.

Thomas jammed the vehicle in 'drive' and stomped the accelerator. "The owner had been growing impatient with the slow progress we were making and when the two men were found dead, he started to get a little antsy about the bad press. It also seems some of the locals had begun to pressure him about all the commotion that was being created, so he had decided to have it all filled back in, donate it to the town, and have it turned into a bird sanctuary or some other such nonsense. He just wanted to be rid of it. So, instead, I made him a late-night cash offer. That man couldn't sign the paperwork fast enough and was utterly relieved to be rid of it."

"You bought it? Where did you get that kind of money?"

"I told you the private sector paid well!" he replied with a grin. "At any rate, it means no one else is involved." Taking her hand, he planted a kiss on her palm. "Please say you will share this with me. I want this to be our legacy together in more ways than one. I can think of no one I want more by my side than you."

Frowning, Cassie looked ahead. "Thomas, I think there is something …"

She was interrupted when they rounded the corner to see bulldozers completely blocking the area, and Parker out in front, speaking with the men in control of them.

Thomas was out of the truck before the dust from the road settled. "What's going on here?"

Parker held a stack of papers above his head. "This is an injunction signed by the local Justice preventing anyone from stepping foot on this property as long as it is still a crime scene," he stepped forward and shoved them into Thomas's chest with a little more force than necessary, "*including* the new owner. Your clandestine middle-of-the-night purchase and subsequent early morning filing of the deed will not override it, Dr. Armstrong," he emphasized.

"You can't do this! It's not legal!" Thomas argued. "This land belongs to me now!"

"And you will have possession of it as soon as the crimes are solved. If you aren't happy with my methods, feel free to take it up with my supervisor. He is, however, on a month-long holiday in the middle of the African jungle on a safari that began this morning. I am almost certain he has no cell reception. In the interim, you might want to find some other way to occupy your time. In fact, it might be the perfect occasion for you to return to London. I have a feeling this investigation is going to be slow and arduous— possibly taking weeks, months, maybe even dragging on for years."

"You will be hearing from my attorney!" Thomas traipsed back to the truck and yanked out his phone. He glared at Parker as he pressed it to his ear.

Cassie wandered over to one of the bulldozers, pretending to be interested in the giant tire but more concerned about Thomas's outburst. It was a side of him she had never seen. "Your doing, I take it?"

Parker sighed. "Two men are dead, and given what you told me last night, I think it best to proceed with an extreme amount of caution! I'm trying my best to convince the Justice to level this place once and for all. No good can come of it."

"So, that's it? A potentially significant historical site will be filled in and lost to the ages, while the deaths of those two men are forgotten right along with it." She started to walk away, but Parker grabbed her by the arm.

"Cassie, let this go. Some things are better left buried, and this happens to be one of them. You of all people should understand that after what you told me last night. There is something unnatural about this place, and you don't need to be psychic or have visions to feel it."

"I never claimed to be psychic, and I am still not convinced what I saw was actual witchcraft. As much as I love the idea that magic exists, my logical mind tells me otherwise. But, let's say, for the sake of argument, there is something evil buried in the middle of that circle. Did it ever occur to you that whatever is out there would be better off in the hands of someone who will treat it with the respect it needs while taking

all the necessary precautions? This whole town knows
what we have been doing out here and if you fill it
back in, they are just going to become more curious.
The rumors will take on a life of their own. I've seen
this happen far too many times. Eventually, you are
going to have every treasure-seeker and devil-
worshiper within five hundred miles out here digging
in the middle of the night and you won't be able to
stop them all. What happens when one of them lays
hands on something like that or worse, someone gets
killed over it? Are you willing to have their blood on
your hands? If—I can't believe I am even saying
this—all this *is* real, whatever is buried out there
needs to be secured so it can't hurt anyone else."

"And how are you going to acquire it if the two men
keeping others *away* from it were seen as threats and
murdered?" he fired back. "How will this thing treat
someone *coming* for it?"

"I don't believe in curses or the boogeyman. I am not
afraid to dig up what's out there," she spat.

"Yet, you have visions—a gift you claim from your
dead grandmother. If that isn't witchy, I don't know
what is. Why can't you just walk away from this,

Cassie? Go back to the States and forget all about this nonsense!"

"I don't think I could if I wanted to!" She glanced back at him over her shoulder. "Please! At least give us a chance to figure out what we're dealing with."

Parker shook his head as Thomas started their way. "No! I'm sorry, Cassie, but I can't let you do that."

"Come on, Cassie. I'll drive you back to my place," barked Thomas. "I have a Zoom meeting with my attorney in an hour and I don't want you out here alone with this man."

Thomas gently slid his arm around her waist and escorted her back to his truck as Parker looked on, a great deal of concern for Cassie's welfare on his face.

Thomas was online and on his phone for the better part of the day, leaving Cassie time to analyze her thoughts. Grabbing a warm blanket, she went out on the back porch overlooking the water and curled up in an oversized chair. Coming out to join her a few hours later carrying two glasses of wine, Thomas had calmed down and immediately took notice of her sullen mood.

"Are you alright? You seem a little quiet."

"I'm fine. I just haven't been sleeping well." She accepted the glass gratefully, glad to see him back to his usual self.

"That is certainly understandable given the circumstances."

"How's it going?"

"My attorney is working on it, but he suggests being patient. Dealing with the SB is much different than the local authorities and they tend to get their way."

She scooched over and he sat down next to her, pulling the blanket to cover them both. "I'm sorry I dragged you out here for a bunch of bureaucratic bullshit. If I had any idea, I would not have involved you."

"Bureaucratic bullshit is just part of the job," she said with a smile. "We should both be used to it by now."

Pulling her against his chest, he kissed the side of her head. "I feel like I have wasted your valuable time. I certainly didn't anticipate all the obstacles that seem to have been placed in our way, but rest assured, we will be making our discovery in no time at all."

"I will admit, it has been the most interesting dig I have ever been on, especially given the fact I haven't dug anything up." She inhaled deeply, the chilly air rolling off the water and burning the inside of her nose, but in a good way. "You know, when you said you had a little fishing shack on the river, I imagined something a little more—'shack-ish'. This is pretty great." She took a long sip of the wine and relished the view. The house was more of an ancient stone cottage by the sea with one bedroom, a large kitchen/living room combo, and a full-wall fireplace that took the chill off nicely.

"It's been in my family for generations."

"You had family here?"

"Oh yes, but that was hundreds of years ago. This place was largely forgotten until I found the deed when going through my mother's papers after she passed. It was falling apart when I took possession of it, so I put in some elbow grease and restored it myself, adding a few modern amenities like wi-fi and running water."

"You did a wonderful job, and I, for one, am grateful you saw fit to add the indoor plumbing!"

His phone buzzed. "Excuse me, I need to take this." He got up and went inside, returning a few moments later with a grim expression on his face.

"Something wrong?"

Thomas scratched his forehead. "That was my attorney calling me back. He made a few phone calls, and it seems there is no Agent Parker with the SB division as he claims."

"What? I don't understand! He collected evidence from the site, had autopsies performed on the bodies, and everything else."

"I'm not sure I do either." Thomas stared down at the screen. "It seems he has somehow convinced the local authorities to do all of the work. At any rate, given the mishandling of the situation, he is confident the shutdown of the site is invalid. My attorney is in the process of lodging an investigation with the SB and said there is no reason we cannot resume work tomorrow morning. With any luck, Agent Parker, or whoever he is, will be in custody come daybreak."

"Why would he do something like that?"

"Treasure hunters? Thrill-seekers? Cosplayers? Who knows?" Thomas brushed the hair back from her face. "But you know what? I don't know and I don't care. Tomorrow, you and I will find out what's out there and possibly make the find of the century," his hand slid over on her thigh, "but tonight, I finally have you all to myself and nothing is keeping us apart. Spend the night with me, hopefully without interruption this time. The past few days have made me realize how much I have missed you, and I think it's time we picked up where we left off."

Cassie powered off her phone before leaning forward and taking his face in both her hands. "I can't think of anywhere I would rather be."

Thomas swept her up in his arms. His lips pressed to hers, he carried her into the bedroom and helped her disrobe. The two took their time, exploring each other's bodies and getting reacquainted.

"That was long overdue," he said and kissed her before pushing the sheets aside.

"Where are you going?" she asked, propping up on one elbow.

"To get another bottle of wine. We've worked up quite a thirst."

As he started towards the door, Cassie caught sight of the tattoos on his back once more. "When did you get those?"

"Get what?" he called back, rattling around in the kitchen.

"The tats! I don't remember you having them before."

"Obviously, you weren't paying attention," he popped his head around the doorway, a bottle of wine in one hand, and two glasses in the other. "I've had those since I was twenty."

"What?" she sat up. "No way!"

"Yes, way!" He grinned, came over, and kissed the tip of her nose.

"What are they?"

"I have no idea!" He shrugged. "Just some old druid symbols I found in a book when I was in college. I thought they were cool."

"Let me have a better look!"

Thomas set the wine aside and took her in his arms. "Forget them! They are just a silly reminder of the folly of my youth. Besides, I can think of something far more pleasant to do than look at my backside."

"Oh really? Like what?" she teased.

"Like this!" Thomas repositioned himself between her thighs and used his tongue to trace a line from her knee to her sweet spot. Her hands threaded through his hair, she found herself lost in the pleasure she was receiving, making the mystery of the tattoos the furthest thing from her mind.

Later that night, Cassie found herself unable to sleep, so she slipped out of bed, careful not to wake Thomas. Pulling on his shirt and wrapping a quilt around her shoulders, she picked up her phone and went out on the porch. Powering it back on, she noticed several missed texts from Parker, the last one being less than an hour ago. It read, *"CALL ME NOW!"*

She hit send and he answered on the first ring. "Cassie! Thank God! Where the hell are you?" he demanded. "Are you with Armstrong?"

"I don't see where that is any of your concern, especially since you aren't even an SB agent. What the hell, Parker—if that is even your name? What are you up to? What kind of game are you playing?"

"Cassie, I can explain everything, but you need to tell me where you are right now so I can come get you!"

"I don't need to tell you anything. I don't even know who you are!" She started to hang up the phone when she heard him say, "There are things about him you don't know!"

"I could say the same about you!" she fired back before hitting 'END'.

Gathering herself, she went back inside and sat down on the raised hearth. The fire Thomas had built earlier had long since dwindled to embers. As she tossed another log on, she took notice of the gray stone that was eerily similar to the ones back at the church. Resting her hand on it and closing her eyes, a brief flash came to her—one of a woman holding her newborn baby, after having given birth only an hour before. She kissed the child on the forehead and handed her to another woman before hanging a satchel over her shoulder and hurrying them out the door. The scene dissolved when she heard Thomas call out from the doorway of the bedroom.

"Did I hear you talking to someone?"

"Phone scammers! They call all hours of the day and night now." She tossed the phone aside. "I couldn't sleep."

Thomas sat down next to her and took her by the hand. "I know the feeling. I'm too excited to see what we will find in the morning. In fact—" he paused as he pondered a thought, "who says we have to wait until tomorrow?"

"It's the middle of the night."

"Yes, and if we wait until the morning, it may take all day to sort through the red tape this man claiming to be an SB agent has created. The land legally belongs to me and there's nothing to stop us."

"It is still a crime scene!" she pointed out.

"Is it?" He kissed both her palms and stared into her eyes. "We don't know what happened to those men. Their deaths could have both been perfectly natural, odd but still, we don't know. For that matter, this Parker fellow may have done something to them to shut everything down so he could get his hands on what's out there for himself. We don't know who he is or what his intentions are. Now that we are on to him, he could be out there at this very moment taking what belongs to us. Come on, Cassie! Can you honestly say you want him to get to it first? I know for a fact you are dying to know what's out there!"

"I don't know!"

"Well, I will never pressure you into doing something you are uncomfortable with, but I'm going to protect what is ours. I really would love for you to come along, but I understand completely if you want to remain here."

Still unnerved by her visions from the rune stones and afraid of what might happen to him out there alone, she reluctantly caved and went to get dressed.

An hour later, they stood in the middle of the circle with several lit lanterns scattered around them, along with a couple of shovels. The excavation site was roped off with police tape, but for some odd reason, no one was standing guard.

"I don't know about this, Thomas. This place is a little disturbing at night," she muttered, reminders of all that she had witnessed coming to mind. Glancing at her watch, she scoffed. "Are you kidding me? It's 3 am—the fucking witching hour?"

"Don't worry, sweetheart, I will protect you!" He took a moment to tenderly press his lips to hers before turning all his attention to the work at hand. Taking a folded page from his back pocket, he held it down close to the light. "The folks with the GPR company emailed this to me earlier today. They took the initial results that were inconclusive before and ran them through a simulation program. With it, they are certain the item buried here is rectangular, roughly two by three feet, and about three feet down."

Cassie glanced over his shoulder nervously when she noticed all the usual sounds of the night had gone completely silent. "That's too small to be another body. What else could it be?"

"There is only one way to find out!" he announced and sank the spade into the soil. The handle reverberated most unnaturally, striking a blow to his right shoulder, and knocking him to the ground.

"Damn it!" he cried out and clutched his arm, rolling over on one side.

"Thomas! Are you alright?" She tossed the tool aside and kneeled to look him over. "Do I need to call an ambulance?"

"No! No! It's just a sprain! I just don't think I'll be able to dig it out like this." He smacked the dirt with his hand out of aggravation, growing even more upset. "Damn it to hell! We are so close! It's right here, within our reach!" He grasped her hand and his beseeching gaze met hers. "Please, Cassie," he implored, "don't let this slip through our fingers! It's far too important to let it go!"

Something deep down inside told her this was not the best of ideas and she hesitated, but after all he had done for her, she couldn't let him down. She WOULDN'T!

"Don't worry, I'll get it!" she assured him and picked up the shovel, a little unsettled by how frantic he had become in such a short period of time. Thomas was usually calm and collected, always the voice of reason with a plan in place. This was a side of him she had never seen before.

Less than an hour later, the spade tip hit something hard.

Thomas moved one of the lanterns closer so they could see better as Cassie brushed off what appeared to be a wooden box. Tugging it free and with the help of Thomas's good arm, they managed to drag it to the surface. The container was of a heavy weight, solid wood, with an ancient Celtic symbol carved on the top—one she did not immediately recognize. As she swept the dirt off with her hand, she noticed it was sealed, but there were no hinges or locks. Turning it on its side for a better look, she was taken aback when a mysterious gust of wind whooshed through, creating an unholy wail in the air as if a banshee had unleashed a deathly howl. The ground beneath their feet began to violently vibrate.

"Get it out of the circle!" ordered Thomas, grabbing her by the arm, and pulling her to her feet with his uninjured arm. "They are trying to stop us!"

"They? Who is 'they'?" she shouted as they started to cross the perimeter, the box clutched tightly to her chest. Looking down, she was astonished to see the skeletons writhing back and forth in their graves. A hand bone shot straight up just as she reached the boundary line and she attempted to bolt over it. Misjudging the height, the digits managed to snag the hem of her trousers, causing her to trip and fall. Tumbling face-forward, her forehead slammed hard against the outside of the box. Blood gushed from her brow and pain slammed into her head.

Trying to focus, she felt as if she had been thrown into an icy vat of water and was drowning, unable to breathe. Before she knew what was happening, her mind emptied and was replaced with a chilling knowledge that sucked the very breath from her body.

The coven had come to the small village from their ancestral home to escape the madness of the witch

hunts overtaking the land. Innocents were being
accused, tried, and put to death with little to no
evidence. The real witches had learned long ago—
the best place to hide was in plain sight. Years of
persecution had taught them to keep to themselves and
become a part of the community, bettering it, and
serving nature as a tribute to the Mother goddess who
sustained them all. Their devotions had been
rewarded with a great amount of knowledge unknown
to anyone outside the circle. The power they wielded
in secrecy ensured the survival of that wisdom and
guaranteed their descendants would be strong in the
years to come. All was well until one member of the
group decided she wanted something that was not
hers.

Millicent Davies, while once a loyal servant, had
become jealous of the coven-leader, Muriel,
challenging her every decision. The others decided
they wanted to live a quiet, peaceful life with those
they had chosen to settle down with. Millicent,
however, wanted nothing but ongoing strife and
unlimited power, even going so far as to exchange her
mortal soul and an eternity serving in Hell, for a

grimoire penned by the Devil himself and a sliver of his seed. She didn't count on the Devil calling for his payment quite so soon.

Millicent had developed a fondness for Samuel Shaw, another woman's husband, and summoned the Devil to possess the man as she lay with him. Driven mad from the possession and the lust left in the wake, Samuel's mind had become addled to the point he attempted to murder his wife, Edith, with his bare hands—and had nearly succeeded. If Muriel had not been at the right place at the right time and intervened with her magic, the poor woman would have surely died.

It was the final straw and the coven gathered, deciding something had to be done, so Millicent was 'anonymously' outed to the town as a witch. During her trial, her former sisters made certain the incriminating evidence presented against her was insurmountable, thereby sealing her fate.

As she burned at the stake, Millicent vowed they would pay for their part in her demise. When her vengeful spirit appeared to roam the land reeking death and havoc wherever possible, they came together to bind her once and for all, entombing her in a box buried on hallowed ground to serve as her prison.

What the coven did not learn until years later, however, was that Millicent had secretly given birth to a daughter, Selena, sired with that sliver of seed from the Devil. The child arrived only an hour before she was tried and burned at the stake and was spirited away by a fellow servant of the Devil to another village, along with the grimoire she had sold her soul for.

Years later, after being raised in the darkness, the daughter returned to exact her revenge upon the ones who killed her mother. Seducing an unsuspecting man, she tricked him into digging up her mother's box so she could absorb Millicent's spirit and knowledge into her own body, strengthening herself and her wrath. The coven's power, however, had grown as well with the addition of their own daughters and the sowing of their good intentions to honor the Mother. The original thirteen witches, led by Muriel, were able to gather enough strength to trap Selena inside a sacred circle, turning her Earthly form to ash, before entombing her spirit and powers inside the grimoire she and her mother both held so dear. It seemed a fitting prison for the two. Unable to destroy it and realizing Selena had placed a spell upon it, only allowing it to be opened by someone with her blood, they decided to ensure the world was never troubled by the mother and daughter again, no matter how steep the price. After creating a deathly pact of their own, the original thirteen voluntarily drank hemlock and lay down in their freshly dug graves, giving their lives to form a protective barrier to act as eternal guardians against the evil within. They would always take care of their own. As an added layer of protection, the box the tome was stored in was covered with an additional spell allowing it to only be opened by the blood of the coven leader's direct descendant, which meant only the combined force of good and evil acting in unison would ever be able to access the power within. The remainder of the coven tearfully raked the soil over their sisters, said their final goodbyes, and returned to the village to carry on with their lives. The families were informed the women were gone, wishing to return to the lands of their ancestors to live the remainder of their lives in the home from which they had come all those years ago. The coven members who were left then went on to raise families of their own, vowing to always have someone nearby watching and waiting in case the evil were to one day ever rise again.

Stunned and confused, feeling as if she were caught between this world and the next, Cassie slowly pushed up on her forearms and forced herself to breathe.

Looking down, she noticed the blood from her wound had dripped onto the carved wood and she watched with bewilderment as the box crumbled to ash and slipped through her fingers, revealing an ancient spell book.

It was then she felt the warmth of Thomas's hands on her shoulder. "Cassie, are you alright?" she heard him say.

Dizzy and unable to speak, she simply nodded and rolled over onto her back. The ground had gone still, and an eerie silence had settled over the area once more.

"Dear God, there it is," she heard him whisper as he kneeled, his eyes locked on the large book, his hand slowly extending.

"Thomas don't touch it!" she warned.

"Oh, I'm going to do much more than that," he muttered and produced a dagger from his belt, his injured arm now completely fine. Closing his palm over the blade, he pulled and dribbled his blood over the enormous book while speaking a few words she did not understand.

"STEP AWAY!" she heard Parker shout, his gun and flashlight raised, aimed directly at Thomas's chest.

"You are too late! You cannot stop me!" Thomas reached for the grimoire. "This is mine by blood and right, and I am taking my inheritance."

"Your inheritance?" Cassie pushed up on one elbow. "What the hell are you talking about?"

"This precious book belonged to my ancestors. I have been searching for it for years and, finally, I have found it!"

"Leave it where it is, or I will shoot!" Parker moved closer. "Cassie, you need to come over here where you are safe."

"Well, this is quite the predicament, isn't it?" Thomas's hands hovered over the book as he weighed his options, his eyes darting to it, Cassie, then to Parker, and to the dirk in his hand.

"Don't make the wrong choice here," Parker advised, inching closer. "You can walk away from this whole thing. I will let you get in your car and go, and I won't come after you if you leave Cassie and the book where they are. It's a good deal after all the crimes you have committed."

After a tense moment of pondering his choices, Thomas made his decision. He grabbed Cassie by the arm and jerked her to her feet and in front of him as he stood. He then placed the dagger to her throat. "Those options are just not going to work for me! You see, I happen to know she means more to you than she does to me right now, especially given the fact her blood has already opened the first seal for me. From where I'm standing, killing her can only work to my advantage."

"Me? My blood? What are you talking about?"

He yanked her head back with a handful of her hair and kissed the side of her face, a malicious grin on his lips, all the while with his eyes locked on Parker who tightened the grip on his gun. "Since the death of your father, you *are* the last descendent of the original coven leader and now that you have done your part, I don't need you anymore. While I must admit, the sex was amazing, I daresay that with the ultimate power of the book in my hands, I will be able to have any woman I desire. You are a liability at this point to me, but Parker over there would be devastated if anything happened to you on his watch."

"The only descendant of the coven leader, but not the coven!" Jessie's voice came from just to their side out of the darkness. "Let her go, asshole!"

"Fucking witches!" grumbled Thomas. He pulled Cassie tighter against him and dragged the blade down her throat and chest. "Well, given how concerned the two of you are about her, I am willing to bet you need her to stop me! That makes this choice easy."

In the blink of an eye, he plunged the blade into Cassie, landing just below her breastbone, before shoving her forward.

"NO!" shouted Jessie and Parker in unison, both rushing forward to catch her before she hit the ground face down, which would have caused the knife to embed in her chest further. Thomas seized the opportunity to grab the grimoire and disappear in the commotion.

Parker gently laid her on her back and shined the flashlight down as Jessie ripped open her shirt to examine the wound.

"Stay with us, Cassie! We can't lose you now that we have found you!" ordered Jessie, touching her now ghostly white face. "We need to get her back to the house!"

Parker holstered his gun, gathered her up, and carried her to the car, all the while keeping an eye out for Armstrong, but the man was gone.

Cassie woke up sometime later in a dark room, illuminated by candles and with the undeniable smell of medicinal herbs and smoke all around her. As she started to come around, she realized she was lying on a small bed in a strange place. Pain shot through her chest when she shifted, trying to raise up, and she cried out.

"Hey! Hey! Easy there!" Jessie gently eased her back down with a firmly pressed hand to her chest, looking on with worry. "You did just take a dagger to your mid-section."

Tears streaked down the sides of her face, and she struggled to form thoughts and words. "What's happening?"

"The essence of it? Dr. Thomas Armstrong bad— coven good!" replied Parker, from just off to her left. Letting her head roll to that side, she closed her eyes; he smoothed her hair back. "Is it safe to assume you had some sort of vision when you touched the box?"

"More than that! It was like watching a long movie in extreme fast-forward, having to take it all in the span of just a few seconds. I got the gist, but I am having trouble connecting a few of the dots."

Jessie brought over a cup of something and helped her to sip it. "We were able to piece together late yesterday that your friend Thomas is the last direct descendent of Selena Moor, the daughter of Millicent Davies, two extremely powerful witches from the late 1500's."

"I sort of figured that one out when he stabbed me, but what was that part about me again?"

"You are the last living direct descendant of Muriel Saunders, the coven leader from that era," replied

Parker. "Jessie and I, along with Ilene over there," the older woman from the museum waved, "are also three who are directly descended from the original members of the thirteen witches you found buried out there. There have always been a few of us around sort of keeping an eye on things."

"Bang-up job," she smarted.

"I told you to quit digging up that stuff," chided Ilene. "You should have listened to me!"

"Touché!" Cassie lifted her head a bit. "Next time, try putting a little more emphasis on the 'evil witch' part." She looked to Parker. "You lied about being an SB agent."

"No, I did not. I just belong to a lesser-known branch that deals in the not-so-well-acknowledged cases. When Jessie called and said an archeologist was digging around after a contractor found some remains, I dropped everything else and made my way out here. We had no idea who Dr. Armstrong was at that time because there was no record of Selena Moor ever having a child of her own. Like her mother, she made sure to keep the lineage hidden well, but after putting two and two together, it was the only explanation. At first, we thought the contractor had just stumbled upon the site by mistake and figured we would tie him up with enough red tape until he just let it go—and we *had* convinced him to fill it back in and to donate the land."

"Then why did he sell it to Thomas?"

"He didn't. I tried to track your phone to get to you, but you had turned it off. You see, when I was trying to find you earlier, it was because the owner of the land had been found dead—you just didn't give me the chance to finish what I had to say. The deed signed over to Armstrong was confirmed as a forgery."

"Thomas killed him?" `

"Yes, and I am afraid it is not the first time he may have committed murder. It goes back much further than you know."

"What? Who else?"

Parker and Jessie exchanged uneasy glances.

"Maybe this part can wait until you are feeling better," suggested Jessie.

"Tell me!" Cassie demanded, her emotions becoming overwhelming. "This is not the time to be keeping any more secrets!"

Jessie took her hand and held it tightly as Parker explained.

"Bear with me. The information has been coming fast and furious over the past day or so, and we are still playing 'catch-up' ourselves. Once I tugged on the right string, it all began to unravel at a rather accelerated pace. When I was conducting basic checks after the deaths of the security guards, something about Dr. Armstrong's past didn't set well with me at all, so I started looking a little deeper and some interesting things presented themselves." Parker exhaled sharply. "Let's go back a bit. Were you aware your friend Thomas did not quit his job with Stanford all those years ago but was instead dismissed under special circumstances?"

"No, that's not right! His mother became ill and needed him to return home to handle her affairs."

"His mother died three years before he went to California."

Cassie was stunned. "That can't be right. Why would he lie about something like that—and why would they have fired him?"

"I spoke with Bethany Giles's mother two days ago and she recalled being on the phone with her daughter at around the time of her accident. Bethany was upset because she had been seeing someone who worked for the college and found out some rather disturbing information about the man. She was on her way to see you to talk about it when the accident happened. Your friend never gave her mother a name, and when she saw how devastated you were at the funeral, she decided it was for the best to just let it go and not mention it. A formal complaint against Dr. Armstrong was discovered buried in a pile of paperwork on the dean's desk a few days later, signed by Miss Giles and dated the day of her death. Given the circumstances, they chose to handle it internally and quietly. I was also able to confirm the man was not invited to your school to teach as he led everyone to believe but instead called in a myriad of favors to get that particular teaching position. He came there because of you."

Cassie suddenly felt ill. "Oh, God! Do you mean to tell me, he has been watching me all my life?"

"So, it would seem now that the other details have emerged. I was only able to connect his lineage to Millicent and Selena when I stumbled across his name on the title to that house out by the water when I was checking the signatures on the forged deed. Something told me his ownership of a place in this sleepy little town was too much of a coincidence. Referencing some old journals and comparing the earliest maps of the area we have stored here, it became clear that the place had been Millicent's original homesite. It all just clicked into place from there."

His face suddenly became strained.

"What else?" she asked.

Clearing his throat, he took a moment and chose his words carefully. "Cassie, I requested a copy of the police report of your friend's car collision. According to the authorities, there was no record of any such accident on that day or even around that time. There was a report, however, of an abandoned car belonging to Bethany being picked up by a tow company at a parking spot overlooking a cliff near the school three days after her 'death'. It was never claimed and was sold at auction two months later. Since no one reported her as missing, no foul play was suspected, and the police didn't get involved."

Cassie shook her head vigorously. "No! NO! Her car burst into flames, and she died instantly. The accident was so horrific, and she was burned so badly, she had to be cremated."

"I think you need to ask yourself WHO told you that is what happened to her?"

"Thomas—he handled everything from dealing with the police to the—" she paused, dumbfounded, "to the funeral home and was even the one—to organize the transportation of her ashes back to her parents—" she trailed off, her mind reeling.

"I spoke to one of the officers who worked in that area at the time. He said where the car was found was a remote spot and an ideal place if someone wanted to…" he stopped and looked at Jessie, clearly not wanting to say the words aloud.

"Ideal place for what?" whispered Cassie, part of her needing to hear him say it and the other part not wanting to believe it.

Parker closed his eyes. "To dispose of someone."

Cassie curled on one side. "I think I am going to be sick!"

Jessie reached for the nearby trash can that held the bloody rags she had used and held her hair back as she vomited.

She cried uncontrollably for several minutes before attempting to compose herself by focusing on something else.

"Where are we?" she asked, sniffling, and wiping her mouth with the back of her hand when she got a look at her massive cave-like surroundings.

"Beneath the inn," replied Jessie, wringing out a wet cloth and wiping her face. "This was the original meeting place of the coven and why the land has been in my family's possession for so many years. It is also where we keep our most sacred secrets." She nodded to a stone altar that held an even larger grimoire than the one from the field—this one having a light-colored leather cover as opposed to the other one that was as black as night.

"What will he be able to do?"

Ilene stepped forward. "That book that is now in his hands contains the darkest magic to ever be unleashed in this world. It was written by the hand of the Devil himself and it binds the essence of the Devil's own child, not to mention it has had generations to gather power. There isn't much he *won't* be able to do and once that damned book gets a true grip on his soul, there is nothing he will not aspire to attain."

Cassie noticed a wall of shelves covered in miscellaneous items. "What's all that stuff?"

"That 'stuff' is a hundred years of my SB division's work." Parker wandered over to it. "Millicent Davies and Selena Moor were not the only ones to make deals with the dark side and these items all hold a certain degree of evil magic, like the items used in possessions, spellcasting, government uprisings—you name it. We hunt it down, take it out of the world, and bring it here, to this natural salt cave, where it is neutralized and removed from the grasp of those who would use it to bring harm to others. It is also why the SB cannot 'officially' recognize me as an agent, even though I 'unofficially' have the entire agency at my disposal."

"How do we stop him?" she asked quietly, anger starting to pull her thoughts together.

Jessie crossed her arms and toed the ground with her shoe. "I am not sure we can. When our numbers were many and the bloodline strong, it would not have been an issue, but now, our world is much different."

Cassie pressed her hand to her midsection and sat up. "Can someone tell me how I survived this?"

Parker smiled, grateful she was at least upright. "Jessie over there inherited some of her ancestor's healing powers and potions. Evita Rogers was the town midwife."

"And it helps that this cavern has some restorative abilities in itself," added Jessie with a half-smile. "I am not sure how it works but people get remarkably better in record time when they rest in here."

"What about you two? What did your grandmothers do?"

"Well," Ilene looked to the book, "my ancestor was Alice Rogers. She was more of the record keeper of the coven. I keep the familial ball rolling by adding pertinent information as it comes along and trying to organize the massive amount of information that is already here."

"And I was the product of Janey Brown," explained Parker. "She watched over the sacred coven items and made sure they were kept safe." Looking at the wall, he shook his head. "I suppose the apples don't fall far from the proverbial trees, do they?"

"Are we safe from Thomas here?"

"Yes! Don't worry about that!" assured Jessie. "Even if he knew about this place, it is warded against evil."

"In theory," Ilene grimaced, "but he is holding a great deal of power in his hands, and we aren't sure what he will be able to do with it. We are flying blind here in case anyone hasn't noticed, so we cannot say for sure."

"Who would know the most about how to handle this?"

"You?" suggested Parker. "You are, after all, the only descendant left of Muriel Saunders. I don't suppose you have any ideas?"

"How about you give me five minutes to digest all this? You know, after I get over the part about having the man I was in bed with just a few hours ago, stab me and leave me for dead!" she retorted.

"So, you and he WERE close," Parker declared with a tinge of disgust.

"Really?" chimed Cassie and Jessie at him in unison.

Jessie reached over and smacked him behind the ear. "Can you not kick the poor girl while she's down? Men!" she scoffed, rolling her eyes before turning back to Cassie. "Muriel Saunders was not only the leader of this coven, but she also happened to be one of the most powerful good witches to ever walk the Earth since the beginning of time. Her accomplishments are legendary, especially given she was able to do them all while successfully passing herself off as a mere village housewife. If we only had a way to tap into her knowledge, we might be able to come up with something."

"What about your visions?" asked Parker. "Would one of Muriel's items be enough to get a read on something?"

Shifting so she was in a more upright position, she shook her head. "I normally only see what has already happened with the item I hold in hand, but I have to admit, the past few have been unusual and a great deal stronger. I'm not sure if there is any way to make adjustments to gain additional information or not. Of course, all of this is a little new to me."

"Wait!" Ilene's head snapped up and she rushed over to the grimoire. "I just remembered something. I seem to recall a spell in the book that was put in place to be used only in the darkest of times. I think this might qualify." Flipping through the book, to almost the beginning, she licked her finger and thumbed through as the others went over to join her. "Here it is. Maybe you can get a vision from it, or we could even try casting it, though there is a great deal of risk in not knowing what it might conjure."

"I guess it's worth a try." Cassie tossed her feet over the side of the bed and tried to stand, wobbling a bit. Parker rushed to her side and caught her before she fell.

"After you have rested and healed," insisted Jessie. "Here, drink some of this tea." Cassie took a sip from a mug that was raised to her lips before pushing it away.

"She's right," agreed Parker. "I saw what that other vision took out of you and that was before you were injured. We will wait until you are stronger and then we will decide what to do."

"So, are we the only ones left?" she asked as Parker settled her back onto the bed.

"I am sure there are plenty of descendants out there scattered to the four corners of the world who are completely unaware of who they are," replied Ilene. "You are just looking at the three families who chose to never move away from the area."

"I certainly had no idea," muttered Cassie, exhaustion starting to overtake her.

"That may have been more out of design, to protect Muriel's lineage in case this day ever came," pointed out Jessie as she spread a blanket across her as her patient's eyes closed. "I have given you something to help you sleep. We can discuss it more when you are feeling better. For now, just rest."

And she did—for twelve hours straight.

"What are you cooking?" asked Parker, sitting down at the kitchen counter, picking up a piece of carrot Jessie just chopped and popping it in his mouth.

"I thought I would make some soup for Cassie when she wakes up."

Parker leaned to one side and noticed the extra-large pot on the stove. He had come to learn over the years that the greater the amount of stress Jessie was experiencing at the time, the larger the batch of whatever she was cooking would be. "Exactly how much do you think she is going to be able to eat by herself?"

"What?" Jessie glanced over her shoulder and winced. "Oh! Well, I can always freeze it...along with the three loaves of bread in the oven…and the chicken I roasted…and the cookies that are cooling."

"Or you could feed the entire town for the next month," he teased.

Parker got up and opened one of the cabinets, taking out a bottle of whisky and two glasses. Filling them to the top, he kept one for himself and handed the other to Jessie before sitting back down. "We almost lost her tonight."

"I know," she said quietly and sipped from her glass.

"I keep asking myself if we should have brought her into the fold sooner. If we had, maybe this could have been prevented."

Jessie laid her hand over on his. "We didn't even know Armstrong existed. There was certainly no way we could have known he had his hooks into her as far back as he did."

"God, I have never in my entire life wanted to rip someone apart as much as I did him tonight. When he ran that blade into her, my heart stopped."

"Mine too!" Jessie looked over at her old friend and smiled, knowing there was a reason he was so upset. "She is pretty easy to fall in love with, isn't she?"

Parker's eyes widened, and he became flustered. "I

never said anything about falling in love with her. I just meant—you know—I'm not the type—and I have only known her a few days!"

"The fact that the mere mention of the subject agitates you to this extent speaks volumes, and you forget who you are talking to. I know you better than anyone," Jessie chuckled, "and my intuition is never wrong. It is screaming out to me that you have fallen hard for her."

"As if!"

"When was the last time you went on a date anyway?" she asked.

Parker thought for a moment. "I believe it was 2009. You remember my ex-wife, Cindy."

"You haven't shagged anyone since 2009?" she exclaimed. "No wonder you've been all grumpy and out of sorts lately."

"That's not what I said, and that is not what you asked. You asked when I last went on a date. There's a difference. Besides, you know I don't have time for socializing in my line of work. Having a significant other is not feasible given my job, especially when you find out she married you to get to your secrets."

"Ah, but Cassie is not just another woman. She has the heart and soul of a good witch, and she would never do someone she loved like that. It also means you are going to have to dust off some cobwebs and step up your game. Roses, candlelit dinners, and fine Belgian chocolates—the whole nine yards and you had better not fuck this up. I like that girl! I want her to hang around for a while!"

Parker swirled the liquid in his glass. "You are assuming we survive the murdering bastard on the loose and his big, black book with a centuries-old witch, whose daddy also happens to be the Devil."

"Well, if we don't, you won't have to worry about it." She went back to chopping.

Parker reached for a cookie on a nearby plate.

"Speaking of dates, when was the last time you went out on one?"

"I had one a few weeks ago, thank you very much, which is certainly less than eleven years ago. I think, my dear Parker, you may have actually set some kind of record."

Lifting his eyebrows, he asked, "And the last time you got laid?" Biting into the cookie, he made a delightful sound. Jessie's cooking was the best he had ever tasted.

"I *may* have visited a close friend last week," she mumbled.

"Last week?" he exclaimed, seemingly jealous. "I think the last time I 'visited' anyone was well over two years ago."

Jessie wiped her hands on her apron, rested her elbows on the counter in front of him, and took the rest of the cookie from his hand for herself. "For Cassie's sake, I hope you remember how 'it' works, but I am always happy to cook up a little something to help 'enhance' the evening activities if you like."

"That poor girl is lying downstairs recovering from a stab wound and you are worried about 'that'—and what makes you think I need any help in that department?"

Jessie sighed, her tone becoming serious. "I think Cassie is the one who needs the help. Thomas did a number on her, but worse, he played mind games with her for years. No one would blame her if she never trusted another man again." She tapped his chest with the cookie. "She needs someone like you, Parker. You are a good person with a kind heart who is honest and loyal to a fault. No matter how surly and tough you act on the outside, I know you are all warm and gooey like this cookie on the inside. And, maybe, just maybe, you could use someone like her to smooth out those rough edges you've developed over the years."

Right on cue, as if sensing she had awakened, Parker came down carrying a bowl and a bottle.

"Jessie insists you need this soup, but I disagree. I think you need whisky," he explained, balancing them in his hands. "Your choice!"

"Whisky!"

"I had a feeling."

Setting the bowl aside, Parker pulled a chair around and sat down next to her. "By the way, if Jessie asks, the soup was delicious. I will never hear the end of it if she thinks I didn't make you eat it, and being on the receiving end of one of her lectures is not a pleasant place to be. Take it from someone who has spent a great deal of time on the receiving end of her lectures."

He removed the top and handed it to her. She pushed up on her elbows and rested against the headboard before taking a long swig.

"You two are close?"

"I daresay she is probably the nearest thing I have to a sister, but don't tell her that. I will never hear the end of that, either. We grew up together and have been through a lot over the years." He regarded her as he fiddled with his thumbs. "Listen, I—um—I want to apologize for that earlier snark about you and Armstrong. It just sort of slipped out, and it shouldn't have. I'm afraid it's been one of those days, and frankly, I never cared for the man."

"Forget it!" She turned the bottle up again before handing it to him. "God, I am such an idiot! I don't understand how it is that I am supposed to be the descendent of one of the most powerful witches ever, and I could not see him for what he truly was. How did he manipulate and hide all of this from me for so long?"

"Hey, don't beat yourself up, Cassie. Jessie, Ilene, and I have been around this stuff all our lives and we were none the wiser. He comes from a line just as powerful as yours and he has far more experience with it. Besides, he was probably marked."

"Marked? What do you mean by that?"

"Does he have any tattoos or symbols that could pass for birthmarks?"

Cassie thought for a moment and nodded. "Yes, a few, now that you mention it, on his back. I only recently noticed them."

"That makes sense. He purposely hid himself from you and everyone else."

"I guess I make a piss poor excuse for a witch."

"I wouldn't say that," he said before having some of the whisky and handing it back to her. "I have never met anyone able to get a vision the way you do. That is a pretty rare thing, and I think you may be better at it than you give yourself credit for, after all, you had NO training."

"Yet, I wasn't able to save my best friend. The thought of them having a secret affair and then him killing her..." she trailed off as a single tear slipped from her eye, and she brushed it aside. "Why would she have kept something like that from me? We were closer than sisters!"

"You have no way of knowing the reason. More than likely, she may not have had any say in the matter."

"What do you mean?" she asked, her brow furrowed.

"I know you haven't had time to process all of this because, frankly, it's a lot, but perhaps she was under a spell of some sort, convinced that it was best to keep things a secret from you, or maybe he was slipping a potion into her drinks that clouded her mind. There are any number of magical reasons for it and it was probably his well-thought-out plan all along."

"Would he have the power to do something like that?"

"Yes, he would, especially if he were raised in a practicing family, and in all likelihood, he was. Cassie, let's be clear— this man is a master manipulator, with a wealth of dark magic at his disposal and there was no way you could have possibly seen this coming. You know these horror movies where you see these folks in their dark robes, sacrificing babies, and having weird sex orgies—they aren't that far off. I have seen it all and a great deal worse. My SB division has more work than they can handle these days, especially since the turn of this century. The world is a much darker place than you know." He reached over and rested his hand on hers. "But, lucky for us, one of the good ones found her way back to us."

"Did you all know about me?"

"We did," he confessed, "but we have kept our distance. We didn't want to accidentally bring unnecessary attention to you and, up until now, there was no need to intrude upon your life. We knew where to find you if and when the time came. Besides, we are firm believers around here that the universe has its way of putting you exactly where you need to be when you are needed."

Cassie's eyes drifted to the book. "Can I look at that? I mean, am I allowed?"

"Of course! It is as much, if not more, your birthright than anyone else's." He helped her to her feet; she leaned against him for support, and he eased her into a chair at the altar that resembled a desk more than anything. Opening it towards the front, Parker showed her Muriel's family tree from several hundred years before, all the way up to Cassie being listed as the last in the line.

"It says here Muriel married a widowed farmer by the name of Thurston Saunders. He had one daughter before they married, Sadie, whose mother died in childbirth, and they had another together, Constance."

Parker pointed to the dates. "Constance and her husband, Miles Hayden, carried on the family line with five daughters, but there is no record of Sadie ever marrying, having children, or even her death. I always thought it rather odd she was never mentioned again. Perhaps she was not part of the coven?"

"Possibly, or maybe there is another reason." Cassie immediately found herself engrossed in the text.

Parker rested his hand on her shoulder comfortingly. "I will give you some time alone to take a look at this, just don't overdo it. You did get stabbed yesterday after all." Squeezing reassuringly, he added, "You aren't alone anymore, Cassie. We are here for you, and we aren't going anywhere. I will be upstairs if you need anything." He quietly departed; the researcher in her was already at work.

"Parker!" she called out as he reached the stairs. "Thank you— for everything."

He smiled to himself. "You're welcome."

The dark grimoire rested on his small dining table, and Thomas circled it with growing anticipation. Running his fingers over the cover, he could feel an ancient vibration emitting from it as if it had a heartbeat of its own.

"Let's see what you can do," he whispered before using his index finger to flip open the cover. A burst of energy immediately knocked him to the floor. A strange haze rose upward from the pages, ascending and spreading until the mist drew together, taking the form of a stunning, dark-haired woman appearing to have an almost primordial quality about her. Extending her hands before her, she wiggled her fingers, obviously relishing the fact she was corporeal once more. Observing a mirror on the wall, she went over to it and adjusted her raven-black hair. It was striking against her porcelain white skin, perfectly offsetting her scarlet-stained lips. She smiled at her reflection.

"Who are you?" she demanded when she finally took notice of Thomas on the floor at her feet.

Gathering himself and climbing to one knee, he eyed her cautiously. "I am Thomas Armstrong, and that grimoire you just popped out of is my birthright as your direct descendent!"

She glanced over her shoulder at him. "Is that right? You had better not be lying to me!" Her hand shot out and grasped his face, pulling him to his feet as fingernails dug in deep enough to draw blood. Releasing him and licking the crimson from her finger, a slow smile formed. "You are *indeed* of my bloodline! It seems that the helpless, weak boy I gave birth to survived after all. Who would have thought? I didn't expect him the live out the year."

"That's right, he did, and he was raised in the dark ways by the guardian you left him with. He made sure to pass all he learned down through the generations. It is how I was able to find the book and set you free!"

"Tell me, what is the year?" she asked, studying the room intently.

"It is 2020."

Her face darkened and she became enraged. "I have been bound in that book for over four hundred years by those bitches? How dare they!" Her head snapped around. "Are members of the original coven still here?"

"A few of their descendants, yes, but that doesn't matter. I have freed you and now you will help me achieve greatness."

Crossing her arms, she asked snidely, "Is that right?"

"You owe it to our family to do as I say!" he replied arrogantly.

Pursing her lips, she cupped his face tenderly. "Tell me, grandson, what is it you are so desirous of?"

Thomas straightened his back. "I want it all—unlimited wealth, magical power, glory!" The overwhelming zeal was evident on his face. "I want every colleague who has ever doubted me to bow down at my feet and grovel for me to simply acknowledge their existence. I want the most beautiful women in the world on their knees fighting over who will have the honor of pleasuring me for the evening. I want to be filthy, stinking rich so I never have to want for anything for the rest of my life. I want to wave my hand and have whatever I want laid out before me."

"All worthy goals! Is there anything else?"

"I think that is a good beginning!"

Selena leaned forward and brushed her lips against his. "Agreed," she whispered. A broad smile appeared, then slowly faded as she closed her fingers around his face once more, only this time tightening her grip like a vice. Realizing a little too late that his mortal life was in danger, he struggled to free himself and began to plead for mercy.

"Just let me go and we can forget all about this. I will leave and you will never see me again."

"Correct on all points," she affirmed and held him in place. The skin on his face began to burn and bubble, turning bright red. Blisters formed, erupting and bursting as smoke seeped from the pores of his skin. The intense heat spread like poison throughout the rest of his body at a rapid speed. An agonizing howl roared from his lips just before his face melted away, the rest of his skin following, finally giving way to a pile of bones that soon turned to cinders.

In the end, nothing was left of Dr. Thomas Armstrong except his singed clothing and a pillar of ash on the floor.

"I answer to no one," she spat, "least of all a greedy bastard like you!" Turning her attention back to the book on the table, she stared at it until a brilliant idea came to her.

"I can't be trapped in it if it no longer exists!"

Placing her hand on the cover, she recited an incantation that allowed her to absorb all the knowledge and energy from it, making it a permanent, inseparable part of her. When she was finished, it turned to ash. Selena now held all its power within, her form now solid, strong, and ready to begin her new life.

Stepping on Thomas's remains, grinding them into the floor, she went over to the fireplace and took a good look around. Sensing something oddly familiar about her surroundings, she closed her eyes and focused until she received a vision. It was then she realized that this had been the house she had been born in. "Damn, it's good to be home!"

When Jessie and Parker checked on her later, Cassie was leaning back in the chair with her arms folded, appearing greatly disturbed.

"You should be resting," Jessie fussed.

"I am feeling better and, besides, I don't think there is time for that anyway." Her eyes remained focused on what was in front of her as she continued, "I dug a little deeper into this dark grimoire that Thomas has laid hands on, and what I found is not good news at all."

"What do you mean?" questioned Parker.

"Well, from what I can gather from the information here combined with what I saw in my vision," she shifted in the chair to face them, "it's not so much Thomas we have to worry about."

"I don't understand."

"It's not just the power that can be released, but Selena herself, and if she gets out, she will not only have her mother's powers combined with her own but the full ability and intimate knowledge of the book she has been bound to for all these years. Basically, she is like a Molotov cocktail concoction that has been simmering while having ingredients added to it for centuries. The power of two witches, along with the book's knowledge, will make her stronger than anyone ever imagined possible. That's why the thirteen, even in the afterlife, were willing to do whatever was needed to stop her from being released. My guess is that the biblical plagues on the job site were their way of trying to warn us, as were the deaths of those two guards. They knew she would be strong enough to destroy whatever, or whoever got in her way."

"That's a rather sobering thought," remarked Parker.

Jessie's eyes went to the book. "That emergency spell Ilene mentioned is looking better and better by the moment. Any idea what it will do?"

"No! There is no way to know, but as of now, it may be the only ace we are holding." Cassie slowly shook her head. "I'm afraid we are going to have to put a great deal of hope and faith in our ancestors on this one."

Parker's phone suddenly buzzed, startling them all. "It's Ilene," he said before answering it.

"Parker!" she shouted in obvious distress. "Get to the spell and cast it NOW! You have to stop her, and it is your only hope!"

"Ilene, what's wrong? Where are you?"

The sound of the phone crashing to the floor was the only response. He hit the button and placed it on the speaker. "Ilene! Talk to me! What's happening?"

"I will make your coven pay for what you did to me!" they heard a voice hiss.

Ilene began to chant a few words, but they quickly turned into screams. Then came the sounds of what could only be the crunch of shattering bones. The three stared at the phone in horror when the deathly gurgle of someone choking on blood began. "Your miserable mothers murdered me and condemned me to centuries of nothingness," they heard a voice bellow, "and I will repay your wretched kind and this world tenfold."

The phone went dead, and they stood frozen, too stunned to react, until they were moved by the shaking and buckling of the ground beneath their feet. Each reached for something to steady themselves as an explosion that came from the direction of the museum rocked the floor once more.

"She's free and we are out of time!" Cassie declared, scrambling to frantically flip through the book. It took mere seconds, which felt like hours until she was able to locate the spell. Taking the grimoire in hand, she held it open and looked to the others. "It's now or never! This is the one chance we have!" They gathered around it, placed their hands in the center of the page, and recited the words in unison.

8

CHAPTER EIGHT

Cassie blinked, gradually becoming aware of a sweet, flowery aroma surrounding her. As her senses adjusted, she discovered she was lying on her back in the middle of a field of tall clover, her throbbing head resting on the book. Shielding her eyes from the sun, she slowly sat up, her face level with the lavender blooms. Something moved behind her and the vegetation started to part. A wake had formed and was headed in her direction. Slightly disoriented and unsure of what she was about to face, she rolled onto her knees and steadied herself, raising her fists, prepared for a fight.

"Baa!"

"Baa?" she repeated and lowered her hands, confused until the grass parted and she found herself staring into two adorable brown eyes.

Breathing a sigh of relief, she relaxed, letting down her guard. "Not who I was expecting, but I will take you any day," she said and extended a hand to rub the small ram behind his ears. The animal treated that action as less of an invitation to cuddle and more of a threat to his existence. Rearing back, he slammed his tiny head, and two small horns, directly into her chest, knocking her backward and flat on her back.

"Oh, you little fucker!" she groaned and rolled to one side, clutching her breasts. "Did you have to get me right where I just got stabbed?"

"Baa!"

Cassie looked down at the red stain forming on her chest as he came over and licked the side of her face. "I am willing to bet Jessie can make a mean mutton stew."

"Baa! BAAAA!"

"Wait! Jessie?" she called out hopefully.

"Did I hear my name?" Jessie suddenly appeared, towering over her, looking down.

"Yeah, I have a sudden craving for lamb. Know any good recipes?"

"Baaaaaa!" the animal protested.

"A few, but let's save it for a celebratory dinner. I think we have bigger issues right now."

Jessie shooed the creature away and helped her to her feet. Lifting Cassie's shirt, she frowned when she saw the wound had reopened. "We need to find somewhere to get you cleaned up!" Bending over and picking up the grimoire, Jessie shouted out, "Parker? You here? Did you make it?"

"Over here!" An arm shot up from another section of the field, along with the sound of an extended groan. "I am getting too old for this shit. Where the hell are we anyway?" he asked, his head full of ruffled hair popping into view. "This doesn't look like the cave."

"Good question!" Jessie surveyed the area as Cassie adjusted her shirt. "I don't recognize this place. What about you, Parker? Does it look familiar at all?"

He stumbled over to join them. "No, it doesn't, but I don't tend to spend a lot of time in the countryside. The dark ones never take the time to appreciate the beauty and peacefulness of nature. If they did, maybe I could take a few of my vacation days." Seeing the blood, he quickly filled with concern. Fiddling in his jacket pocket, he managed to locate a handkerchief and handed it to her. "Here, use this to put some pressure on that until we can do better."

"You there! What are you three doing with my animals?" they heard someone shout angrily. Turning, they were bewildered to see a peculiarly dressed man, furiously red in the face, storming towards them.

"What the hell is he wearing?" whispered Cassie when she noticed his wool tunic and breeches.

"I'm not sure. It's not exactly the latest in farming fashion though, is it?" replied Jessie in a low tone.

"I ask again—what are you three doing in my field? Have you injured my ram? If you have, you will be paying for him."

"I think you should be paying *me*," mumbled Cassie, wincing as she pressed the cloth to her mid-section.

"No, sir!" replied Parker, placing himself protectively between the man and the women. "We were just out for a walk and lost our way. Our friend requires some medical attention. Could you please tell us exactly where we are, and point is in the direction of the nearest health facility?"

"What are you women wearing?" demanded the man as he approached, averting his gaze and turning his face away. "I will not be having harlots on my land. You need to move along."

"Harlots? Who are you calling a 'harlot'?" snapped Jessie, lunging towards him before Parker caught her around the waist and pulled her back.

"We are God-fearing folk here, and we will be having none of your sinfulness in our village."

"I can assure you—" started Parker, only to be interrupted by another voice.

"Thurston! Who the devil are you hollering at? Good Heavens, you will raise the dead with all that ruckus!"

It was then the three noticed the small cabin on the edge of the field and a woman standing near the front door with her hands on her hips.

"Never you mind, Muriel. This man and his women have stumbled on our land. I was just sending them on their way."

"Muriel?" Cassie turned, angling for a better look at the woman. Her face paled. "That wouldn't be Muriel Saunders, by chance, would it?"

The man narrowed his eyes. "How do you come to know my wife?"

"We might be related?" Cassie squeaked and stared at the woman in disbelief.

Thurston scratched his head. "I can't say I have met any of her kin in all the years we have been married."

Speechless, Jessie and Parker turned to gawk at the woman while waiting for a response.

"They said they might be some of your relations," he called back.

"*My* relations? Well then, bring them here so I can see who they are! A clover field is not a proper place for welcoming family."

"You heard my wife!" Thurston held out his hand in the direction of the house. "What's that you're holding?" he asked Jessie as she clutched the book to her chest tightly.

"Oh, this? It's my—um—" she looked to the others for guidance.

"The family Bible," finished Cassie. "We never leave home without it."

"Well, that's a good thing." Thurston offered an agreeable dip of the head. "Especially with all the witches that seem to be lurking about these days. You can never be too careful or have enough of the good book behind you."

"Holy shit!" muttered Parker as they moved. "It can't be possible, can it? Are we sure Selena didn't get to us and mess with our minds? Maybe this is a dream? Or maybe we are just dead, and this is Hell!"

Jessie reached over and pinched him.

"OW! What did you do that for?"

"We are not in a dream and you're not dead," she said with a wink.

"You're a mean one, you know that?" he muttered, rubbing the spot.

Jessie grinned and blew him a kiss.

"No, that's definitely her," Cassie whispered. "I recognize Muriel from the vision I had. I guess the spell really did send us to the only person who could help us. It just so happens, she isn't alive in our time."

The three followed Thurston inside, stopping to take in every detail of the home. The smell of a wood fire, drying sage, and a hint of beeswax candles greeted them as they crossed the threshold.

Muriel stood with her back to them, stirring something in a pot on the fire. Turning when she heard them come in, she wiped her hands on her apron and gave them a good once over.

"Do I know you?"

Cassie swallowed hard and nervously stepped forward. "No, but I am fairly certain we are related."

Muriel's brow furrowed, and her eyes narrowed when she noticed the grimoire in Jessie's hands. The bewildered older woman's attention turned back to Cassie as she lifted her hand and touched her visitor's face, seemingly as dumbstruck as they were when a strange sensation passed between the two. "Yes, I think we might be."

"Well, do you know her or not?" demanded Thurston who was watching the exchange curiously.

Muriel smiled warmly and wrapped her arms around Cassie's shoulders. "Of course, I do. This is my cousin's girl. I just haven't seen her since she was a child. My dear—" she inclined her head, "what's your name?" she whispered in her ear.

"Cassie," she replied.

"Cassie! Yes, of course. The name was there on the tip of my tongue! She is Rose's girl!"

"Who the devil is Rose?"

"Rose is my cousin! You know that!" Muriel scoffed. "My darling sweet husband, you would forget your own name if I weren't here to remind you."

Thurston scratched his head. "I suppose that is the truth of the matter!" he conceded with a good-natured wink. "I would be lost without you!"

"And these are—"

"My friends," answered Cassie. "Jessie and Parker."

"Thurston, it seems we have some additional company for supper. Why don't you go butcher one of the sheep so I can get it on the spit?"

"Might I suggest the little fuck—fellow in the field?" catching herself as she rubbed her chest. "He looks particularly delicious."

Thurston offered her a peculiar look as he shoved his hat on his head and went out the door.

As soon as he was gone, Muriel turned to the three, her demeanor darkening. "Who exactly are you and what are you doing here?"

They exchanged uneasy glances.

"It might be difficult to explain. I am not sure we understand ours—"

Muriel laid her hand on Cassie's arm, cutting her off. "ONLY THE TRUTH, GIRL!"

The words spilled forth from her lips, out of her control. "I am your many times' great-granddaughter, and we are here because Selena Moor's descendant is causing problems in the future." She then proceeded to quickly relate the entire story from when she first met Thomas in college up until he took the grimoire with all the details in between. When she was done, she shook her head as if coming out of a trance. "Damn! How did that happen?"

"What the bloody hell, Cassie? You just felt the need to blurt that right out," scolded Parker, his eyes wide.

"I don't think I had any choice in the matter!" She looked at the older woman. "Did I?"

"Nay, you didn't! I placed a truth spell on you," Muriel replied, frowning. "You mean to tell me you are from a time far from today? How is that possible?"

"Magic, maybe?" Jessie reached down and picked up the book, shaking it. "Look familiar?"

"Is that—?"

"It is!" Jessie held it out. "It's how we got here, and believe me, we are just as dumbfounded as you are."

"Selena Moor's descendent?" Muriel slowly sat down on a bench at the table, the pieces coming together in her mind. "Well, that is a problem, isn't it?"

"You believe us?" asked a confused Cassie. "Just like that? You have no doubt we fell out of the sky from the year 2020 with this bizarre, completely insane story."

"Oh!" Muriel waved her hand. "Actually, this is not the strangest thing I have ever encountered, and yes, I do believe you. I wrote that spell myself and I know how powerful it can be. If you are here, the situation must be extremely dire. Besides, no one can lie to me when I lay hands on them and command the truth." She sighed. "How did we miss the fact she has a child out there?"

"Out there somewhere, yes, but we don't know any more than that, and we certainly don't know how to find this child," said Parker. "If we did, perhaps we could head this all off at the pass."

"Are you insinuating that if we knew where he or she was, we should just kill them?" asked Cassie.

"Not my first choice, by any stretch of the imagination," he replied delicately, "but you must admit, it would solve our future problems."

"I am not sure that is a plan I can get on board with."

"There is no need to speak of such a thing," interjected Muriel, "for we don't know where this little one is, nor do we have the time to look."

"I take it you have already encountered Selena?" Parker probed.

The older woman lifted her eyes, ones that suddenly appeared weary beyond her years. "We entrapped her in the grimoire just last night. We are currently settling our affairs and making the arrangements to form the circle you speak of," she glanced out the window, "spending the next few days with the ones we love and preparing them for life without us in it. But, if what you are telling me is true, it will all be for naught."

"No, not at all!" offered Jessie, dropping the massive tome on the table, her arms unable to hold it any longer. "Your tremendous sacrifice kept it out of the wrong hands for over four hundred years, and that is no small feat. We, the descendants who remained to keep watch, were the ones who failed. We didn't know anyone like him even existed, and we never saw him coming. But, forewarned is forearmed, and we were sent to you for a reason."

"Your arrival at this time speaks volumes, as well." Her eyes fell to the book. "This certainly has grown quite a bit." Muriel let her fingers glide over the cover. "Why did you bring it with you?"

"We were running short on time, and I was afraid to leave it behind when Selena blew up our friend." Miserable expressions filled the faces of the three when they realized they had not had a moment to grieve Ilene. "If she hadn't warned us, we likely wouldn't have made it out in time."

Muriel patted her hand. "I'm sorry about your friend, dear."

"For the record," Jessie tapped the book, "we told your husband it was a family Bible. He seemed to take comfort in the fact we carried it as protection against all the roaming witches you apparently have around here."

Muriel nearly snorted. "Well, he has always had a fear of witches. The man would shite himself if he knew one had already gotten to him—and married him! One, whom I might add, loves him more than life itself. Fortunately for you, he cannot read." She picked it up and placed it on the bottom shelf of a nearby cabinet. "But let's put this away for the time being just to be cautious."

After concealing it with a few other items, she straightened up and looked at Cassie fretfully. "Is that your blood?"

"Oh yeah! Your little friend outside reopened my wound when he head-butted me."

"The little ram? Oh, that's Herman, and I am fairly sure a meaner four-legged creature was never born into this world. Unfortunately, Thurston adores the little bugger." Muriel pulled her over and made her sit before reaching for a basin of water. Lifting her shirt, she paused when she saw the spot where she had been stabbed. "You were blessed, my dear. A little more to the right and that dagger would have hit you directly in the heart. You would have left this world instantly."

"The thought did occur to me," Cassie mumbled. "Thank goodness these two were there when it happened."

Jessie rubbed her shoulder. "We couldn't let you go so easily, especially after we just found you."

"Mother?"

The group turned to see two young women who had quietly slipped inside. "Father said we have guests. Who are these people?"

"Close the door!"

Constance and Sadie Saunders cautiously eyed the others as they placed their baskets of freshly picked vegetables and herbs on the table and went to her side.

"Are you alright, Mother?" asked Sadie, taking her hand.

"Yes, I am, but you need to hear this." She introduced the group and explained the situation as she cleaned Cassie's wound. The time-travelers were amazed to see how surprisingly accepting of the news the two daughters were.

"We gather in three days to form the circle, so we have that long to figure out a way to help you before sending you back where you belong." Pointing to the cabinet, "Sadie, bring me something to bind this with."

"Any ideas on how we can stop her?" asked Cassie.

"Well, not off the top of my head, but hopefully we can come up with something!" Muriel accepted a bundle from Sadie and started to tear the fabric into strips. "In the meantime, I intend to have one final family supper with the ones I love surrounding me. Parker, perhaps you can go help Thurston and Constance's husband, Miles, with the butchering? What we don't use for today's meal will need to be cut up and hung in the smokehouse."

"Um—" he blew out a breath and uncomfortably looked towards the door, "I guess I can try, I suppose?"

Muriel seemed surprised. "You don't do your own butchering in the future?"

"Not as long as there is a grocery store nearby."

"What's a grocery store?" asked Sadie curiously.

"A place where you can buy meat you don't have to kill or even cut up yourself and fruits and vegetables you don't have to grow. It's like a market with a lot more choices," replied Jessie as she casually peeked into one of the baskets and smiled at what she found. "Go on, Parker. It will do you good to learn a new skill."

"Yes, because I will need to know how to do that back on the farm with Bessie the cow, Peggy the pig, and all the chickens I keep," he replied sarcastically.

"How did you know what I was getting you for Christmas?" she joked.

"Well, do whatever you can do to keep them outside a little longer while we put our heads together," Muriel ordered and sent him on his way. "The women need to talk." Closing the door behind him, she asked, "Which family is he from?"

"Janey Brown's."

"Of course! I should have known. They have the same beautiful eyes, though he is a little bit taller than she is," she said wistfully. "Her daughter just found out she is with child. It's a shame she won't be around when he arrives."

Constance suddenly put her arms around her mother's waist, her eyes becoming watery. "I don't know how we are going to make it without you! Surely, there must be another way! We need you!"

"It is the way of the world, my darling! The old must do their part to serve the Mother, then pass the torch to their children to do the same. I am at peace with what must happen, and I want you to be, as well. Do not grieve for me when I am gone. If I am being truthful, while I will miss you all terribly, I am looking forward to finding out what comes next, especially knowing I will be leaving all my knowledge in the very capable hands of my two beloved daughters."

Cassie and Jessie uneasily locked eyes for a moment, and Muriel took notice.

"What is this?" asked Jessie as she picked up a piece of root with yellow flowers and inhaled, hoping to change the subject.

"That's silphium," answered Sadie, taking it from her, "and you might want to be careful with it. It is rather potent."

"Why? Is it poisonous? I have never heard of it."

"It can be downright deadly in the right hands," Constance pressed her lips together, a gleam in her eye.

"Silphium?" Muriel folded her arms and glared suspiciously at her two daughters. "What the devil are you two up to anyway?"

"Nothing! We just thought you and Father should enjoy the next few nights together," mumbled Sadie, removing a few more herbs and arranging them on the table. "After all, it will need to last him the rest of his life, and you deserve to have a few memorable moments to leave this world with, as well."

"What am I missing here?" questioned Jessie.

"It is an extremely powerful aphrodisiac that enchants the mind." Muriel snatched the plant from Sadie, cocked her head to one side as if pondering the thought, and hastily stuffed it into the pocket of her apron. "I will just store this somewhere safe for the time being. Wouldn't want it to fall into the wrong hands by mistake."

Constance and Sadie grinned at each other behind their mother's back.

Jessie appeared intrigued. "I would like to get a little clipping of that if I could. While I have seen references to it in some very old recipes, I have never actually laid eyes on it. I don't think it even grows anymore."

"You are a healer?" Sadie asked.

"I can hold my own, but cooking is what I love. I think it probably runs in the family. My ancestor is Evita Rogers."

"Then this must be your doing," Muriel said as she started to bind the wound. "You did very well. There is no sign of infection, and it seems to be healing at a remarkable pace." Muriel smiled warmly. "Evita is one of my closest friends! She delivered Constance. She will be thrilled when she learns her legacy lives on for so long in this world. You are going to make her very happy."

"Oh! It just occurred to me that I will get to meet her!" exclaimed Jessie. "We had no idea what the spell would do, much less that it would bring us back in time to all of you, which is crazy because it isn't a thing in the future."

Noticing Cassie's solemn mood, Muriel handed the bowl of dirty water to Constance, indicating with her eyes they needed a few moments alone. "Why don't you three girls go dump this and fetch me some fresh water? Get a couple of jugs of ale from the cellar for later while you are at it." Constance and Sadie took her meaning, seizing Jessie by the arm.

"Can you help us, Jessie?" asked Sadie, steadily guiding her towards the door, giving Muriel and Cassie some privacy.

Cassie rested against the wall and stared blankly through the window as Muriel finished her binding.

"Are you alright?" asked Muriel.

"This is all a little extra strange for me," she said when she finally spoke. "Parker and Jessie knew who, and what, they were growing up, but I never did. No one in my family ever spoke one word of witches or covens and I certainly had no idea I was descended from one. Magic was just something children believed in because it was told to them in fairy tales. I find myself questioning everything I ever believed about everyone I ever knew, including myself."

"You know, being able to call up visions at will is a gift only the strongest of our kind are able to do. Often, these types of abilities will skip several generations, allowing the power to gather into one individual. If you are indeed the last of our line, I dare say you have a great deal of potential within you yet to be discovered. Whether you know it or not, you are very special, Cassie, and you should never question that."

"I don't feel special—I feel more like an idiot. I didn't even know the man I took into my bed had slept with my best friend before murdering her."

"Sometimes, we don't see because we don't *want* to see."

"That makes me even more responsible for all of this. If I had been paying more attention all those years ago, maybe I would have seen what was happening right under my nose and recognized Thomas for the man he truly is. Bethany might even be alive today if I had."

"From what you have told me, and given who he is, this man, Thomas, is a master at the craft, and he knew exactly what to do to gain your trust. Being an empathetic soul and having an open heart is NOT a weakness, but instead, a great strength possessed by precious few." Movement through the window caught their attention and they watched Jessie, Constance, and Sadie laugh over something as silly as carrying a bucket of water. Muriel beamed. "Know this, Cassie, some things never change, even with time. The strongest magic in the world is, and always will be, love. As long as you have that in your heart, guiding your conscience and your actions, you will never be led astray."

"I may not be much of a witch or know how to save anyone, but I am one heck of a researcher and what I found out might help you save someone YOU love. I spent a great deal of time going over that book and you might want to take a look for yourself." Cassie sniffled. "I am not sure if it means anything other than the recordkeeping got behind, but it says Constance is the only one to carry on the family line. There is no mention of Sadie after her birth."

"Is that right?" Muriel let out a heavy sigh, turning to look her up and down. "Perhaps, you WERE brought here for more than one reason, but first things first.

Come on, child, let's find you something clean and
decent to wear before my husband has an apoplexy."

Within an hour, both Cassie and Jessie found
themselves trying to figure out how to get into the
long, coarse dresses and aprons Muriel had laid out
for them.

"Dear God, this thing is itchy!" complained Jessie,
raising her arm to smell the material. "When do you
think this was washed last?"

Cassie shrugged, using a small looking glass to see
how she looked. "Who knows? It doesn't do much for
the figure, does it? I guess we won't be modeling in
any spring fashion shows."

"Just be glad we had on bras and underwear. Can
you imagine how rough this would be without them?"
Jessie chuckled. "I will never take cotton t-shirts or
sleeveless summer dresses for granted ever again!"

After they finished changing, they pitched in with
the cooking, finding it quite an ordeal in the current
century. After hours of work preparing one meal, the
group enjoyed an early afternoon dinner. Thurston
was full of questions about them, and each time he
asked one, the three would simultaneously stuff a

piece of bread in their mouth to avoid answering. Muriel obviously had years of experience distracting her husband and she easily shifted the topic of conversation in another direction whenever he became too inquisitive. The rest of that day was spent putting meat in the smokehouse and preparing days of food for Thurston after Muriel's departure. Whenever Thurston and Miles were out of earshot, Muriel and Cassie would speak in hushed tones, getting to know each other better, and questioning the other about her life. By the end of the day, it felt as if they had known each other all their lives.

Later that evening, with their bellies full after a supper of leftovers, Cassie, Jessie, and Parker were offered the barn for the night given the fact the house was too small for so many people. They were just getting settled when Sadie came in carrying a lantern.

"I brought some blankets for you, and there is more ale over here, as well. We don't usually have company, so I don't have much to offer."

"This is perfect and very kind of you!" Jessie spread one out on the floor as Sadie brought over two jugs.

"It was a good reason to get out of the house. Constance and Miles went home, and I normally sleep in the loft above my parents' room. Given the sounds coming from below, I can only assume Mother slipped a great deal of that silphium into Father's ale. I thought it best to give them some privacy."

"Oh!" Jessie covered her mouth with her hand and giggled. "In that case, we are happy to have the company. No one should have to listen to their parents doing THAT!" The two young women shared a good laugh.

Sadie and Jessie soon found themselves lost in their conversation. Sadie was excited to hear about the future, while Jessie was happy to learn more about some of the customs of the time. Cassie and Parker looked at each other awkwardly when they began to feel like they were intruding. Parker pointed and quietly motioned to the door. The two slipped out unnoticed for some fresh air, taking one of the jugs with them, and rested against the side of the barn, gazing up at the stars.

"It's so strange to see this place without things like electricity lighting homes, cellphone towers, and even airplanes flying overhead," remarked Parker. "It's eerily quiet with the 'hum' of the modern-day world just gone. I can't say I dislike it."

"When I am out on excavation sites at night, occasionally it gets like this. I will sometimes take something we have dug up in hand just to let the vision of life at that time wash over me. It's an amazing thing to experience but being here like this in the actual time—well, there is simply no comparison. It's just so peaceful."

"You are right about that!"

"Do you think we have any chance of stopping Selena?" she asked quietly as they shared the ale.

"Well, if you had told me yesterday that we would be having roast mutton in the sixteenth century with one of the most powerful witches in history, I would have called you insane, yet here we are. I suppose anything is possible. And let's not forget, we do happen to now have a skillful coven in our corner. I would say our chances are much better than they were before we recited that spell."

"Yeah, I guess you are right. It's too bad we didn't say it before Selena got to Ilene."

Parker reached over and tenderly slipped his hand into hers. "I know you blame yourself for all of this, but none of it is your fault. The responsibility for this mess lies squarely on Armstrong's shoulders and no one else."

"I keep going over everything in my head, trying to figure out how I could have missed this thing with him and Bethany. The three of us were the best of friends and to learn he killed her? And for what? Just to get close to me? I don't believe I have ever hated anyone in my entire life, but when I think of him now, my heart goes to a very dark place."

"Don't give him that much power over you, Cassie. If you do, he wins, and we are not going to let that happen. We can't!"

Cassie leaned her head on his shoulder. "Let's not talk about him anymore tonight. I just want to enjoy the calm before the storm."

"I think that sounds like a wonderful idea!" Gripping her hand tightly, he asked, "How are you feeling? After all, you did get stabbed yesterday and butted by a ram this morning."

"Oh yeah, thanks for reminding me," she groaned before lifting her hand and touching her wound.

"Believe it or not, it feels pretty good. I think Muriel may have worked a little of her own magic on it."

"I am just grateful you are here and in one piece." His eyes drifted down to hers and his gaze lingered. Cassie shifted to face him better as the two found themselves inexplicably drawn to each other. Slowly coming together, they were soon absorbed in an intense, passionate kiss beneath the beauty of the stars. They were interrupted, however, by the rather unmistakable sound of an amorous couple in the throes of passion coming from the direction of the house. Parker rested his forehead against hers and they shared a laugh. Putting his arm around her shoulders and pulling her closer to him, he said, "You know, I thought, in my line of work, I had truly seen it all, but apparently, I was wrong. Muriel seems very much—" he paused, searching for the words.

"Like an ordinary person?" Cassie finished for him.

"Yes! Exactly! Of all the stories passed down over the years, I imagined Muriel Saunders to be some sort of ethereal, magical being who perched over the world, keeping watch and holding the darkness at bay."

Cassie winced. "Yet, here she is, feeding her

husband roofies," they looked to the house where the loud noises were emitting from, "and cold banging his brains out as one of her final wishes on Earth. She seems pretty much like the rest of us poor bastards, doesn't she?"

"That is an accurate way of putting it." Parker grinned. "I must admit, I feel a little letdown. I was expecting more in the way of black cats, the eyes of newts, and the pricking of thumbs, not to mention that the cauldron hanging over the fire isn't nearly big enough for brewing up potions and calling up storms. Every illusion I had in my mind as a child has been shattered!"

"Maybe that is what the cave is for," she said with a chuckle. "In my mind's eye, I can see it all now—a Halloween setup that would put Martha Stewart to shame."

"It's good to see you laugh, Cassie. I would like to see a great deal more of it."

She looked down. "Lucky for you, I think it comes right before the complete mental break, so I should be right on schedule for your evening entertainment purposes."

"Thanks for the warning! You know if you take away Selena, the madman in the future, the evil grimoire in their possession, and all that can go wrong, the fact that an archaeologist and an SB agent are sitting here experiencing life in a way no one else ever will is pretty amazing when you think about it."

"An archaeologist and an SB agent walk into a barn—sounds like the beginning of a bad joke, doesn't it? Only, the joke is on us!" Her eyes shifted to the sky. "But you're right. I really should be taking in more of this from a professional aspect. I mean, who else in the twenty-first century will ever be able to say they lived the life of a sixteenth-century person?"

"Maybe that's what is so special about these women and why they are so legendary within our circle—they accomplished all they were able to despite being just ordinary human beings. If that is the case, maybe it will bode well for the rest of us."

A cool breeze picked up and Cassie shivered. Parker stood and helped her to her feet. "Come on, it's getting late, and you are still recovering. Let's get you inside where it is a bit warmer so you can get some rest."

Before he opened the barn door, he hesitated, bending to kiss her once more. Cassie gingerly pressed her hand to his chest, preventing him from going any further. "Maybe this isn't such a good idea. Things are a little complicated and, after Thomas, my head isn't in the best of places. I have a lot to work through before I can even consider what comes next. I'm sorry."

"I understand completely," he replied, the disappointment evident in his voice. "We should go inside and get some sleep. We don't know what tomorrow will bring."

He pulled open the door and followed her inside. Jessie and Sadie were already asleep, so they slipped in quietly and settled for the night.

In the early morning, near the witching hour, Cassie found herself unable to sleep. Slipping out of the barn, she noticed a candle burning in the window. Muriel looked up from the table at that same moment as if sensing her presence and waved her inside.

"It is a very strange thing to see the book as large as it is," she said to Cassie, who quietly closed the door behind her.

"I think a lot of people have been contributing over the years."

"Do you know the saddest part about all this business?" Muriel seemed nostalgic as she rested her forearm on the opened book. "Millicent wasn't always the way she was at the end. In fact, she and I grew up together and were the closest of friends. When we fled our original home with the others because of the witch hunters, we all agreed to make quiet new lives for ourselves, free from persecution—and we did. This village welcomed us with open arms and took us in as if we had lived here our entire lives. We settled in, quietly protected our neighbors, and started families. We were happy."

"What happened?" Cassie took the seat across from her, pulling a borrowed shawl around her.

"What is the one thing behind every woman's fall from grace? She fell in love with the wrong man."

Cassie scratched her forehead. "I suppose I can relate."

"When we first arrived, she married a man she loved dearly. His name was Carl, and they were incredibly happy together. Soon, she became with child, but the birth was difficult, and their son did not survive. Millicent conceived again and lost that boy, as well. Still, she persevered and came to her coven sisters asking for help with a spell to give her a child, which of course, we readily agreed to. We waited until Carl needed to travel to the next village over and made our plans, but at the last minute, I had to delay because Thurston became extremely ill, and I could not leave him alone. The following week, we tried once more and spent the entire day getting the ceremony ready for his return, but when suppertime came and went and Carl had not come home, Millicent grew frantic with concern as did the rest of us. His body was found the next morning, his cart having overturned and crushed him beneath. As a community, we came together and did all we could for her, but her mind was never the same again. It was then that the neighbor, Samuel Shaw started to check in on her, being concerned for his widowed neighbor living alone. He and Millicent began an affair, but when he tried to end it, her mind was unable to handle another loss. We had no idea what she was up to until it was too late, casting a spell that brought in the Prince of Darkness himself. She made a deal and never looked back, seducing Samuel, offering his body up as a vessel for the Devil to visit her for that one night. The act addled poor Samuel's mind for months afterward, becoming worse by the day until he could think of nothing but her. When his wife tried to reason with him, he beat her to within an inch of her life and would have completed the job if I had not been returning from a meeting with the coven at the same time. I was able to lift the blinders from his eyes and when he saw what he had done, he became so distraught, he walked straight out into the stream and drowned himself that very night. Millicent blamed me for it all and demanded I step down as leader of the coven, even going so far as to try and convince the others that dark magic was better for them than the light. When no one rallied to her side, she became enraged, taking vengeance on her own, casting spells to make animals fall dead, causing crops to fail and people to die. It went on for months. The villagers needed someone to hold accountable and she needed to be held responsible. Turning on one of our sisters was the hardest thing I have ever had to do, even more so knowing at the core of all of it was the fact she was simply a woman who had her heart broken one too many times." She paused and let out a burdened sigh. "I often wonder how differently things might have gone had I left Thurston's side the night he was ill to cast the spell. If Millicent had conceived by Carl the week before he died, she would have at the very least, had a child to love and cling to. That alone could have made all the difference."

"There is no way you could have known," Cassie touched her arm, "and you can't blame yourself for what happened. You were taking care of your husband, as any good wife would have done."

Muriel grasped her hand. "The same way you couldn't have known about the motivations of a man you had never met before, especially when you didn't even know who you were. We can only act with the knowledge we have in front of us at the time, not of what we will come to learn after the moment has passed."

"Point taken!" Cassie conceded.

"*If* we had known she had conceived a child of darkness, we would have moved to do something sooner, but we did not, and had to deal with the aftermath."

"How did you find out about her?"

"Selena Moor hit our village hard and fast. Before we had a grasp on what was happening, she had murdered two of the original thirteen's daughters, caused almost half of the crops to turn to rot in the field, and sickened nearly thirty with fish caught from our waters. She finally revealed herself to me when I returned home to find her in bed trying to seduce my husband with a spell she had cast over him. Selena wanted me to know she held me personally responsible for what happened to her mother."

"What a bitch!" muttered Cassie.

"Indeed! While she was very powerful indeed, she had not counted on the fact that we had secretly grown the strength of our coven to nearly forty, from the addition of our daughters alone. I offered up myself to her to do with as she wished, provided she left the others alone. Setting a pre-appointed time and place to meet, she was so focused on revenge, that she never suspected we were laying a trap for her and didn't see it coming until she was caught by the rune stones in the circle. We knew we had only precious moments before she was able to free herself from it, but it was enough time to douse her with whisky and set her flesh afire. As her body perished, we contained her spirit in the book, where it lies now being watched over until we form the final protective circle."

"The one that holds perfectly fine until I come along and release her. I don't suppose you can write up a spell and send me back in time to make a career change in college?"

"I am afraid not. What was done before you came here cannot be undone, and you will be returned to the moment you left, but we don't have to send you back completely empty-handed."

"You have a plan?"

Muriel looked towards the door. "Not so much that, as an observation. I have noticed from the recordings in this book that the coven's power has greatly weakened throughout the years. While your friends may have certain inclinations and are able to sufficiently cast a spell or two, they wield no real power because they don't live as our coven does now. What has happened to our magic in your world? Why was it not passed in practice the way it was always meant to be?"

"Yeah, 'magic' as you call it, is not a thing in the future. I mean we have people who practice Wiccan, both good and bad, but they are few and far between. No one lives like that anymore because no one believes in it—including me up until a few days ago."

"That could be a problem, and a bigger one than you know."

"What do you mean?"

Muriel frowned. "Selena is a powerful witch in her own right given her parentage and the grimoire she possesses, but add in the fact she has been buried with it for over four hundred years…"

"She's been brewing and stewing in her own juices for centuries," Cassie recalled the information she read in the book, "having nothing else to do but gather and perfect her powers."

"And our line has been greatly weakened. We were strong enough to take her on a night ago with a full practicing coven, but with only three of you and no power—"

"What you are saying is that we are completely fucked!"

Muriel screwed up her face and placed her hand on her hip. "Do all women speak in such a crude manner in the future?"

"When the occasion calls for it, and I think this is one of those times."

Muriel pursed her lips. "Well, you very well may be...*fucked*!" Both hands flew to her mouth, and she chuckled behind them. "Oh! I had no idea saying that word aloud would be so—so—"

"Gratifying?" Cassie finished for her. "Especially when there isn't anything else you can do."

"Oh, my dear, I never said THAT!"

"Muriel? Where are you, my love?" they heard Thurston call out.

Grasping her hand, she looked towards the door. "It will be morning soon. You and I both should get some sleep. Tomorrow, we figure out how to save your future."

After a breakfast of bread and cheese, Muriel sent Thurston to Constance's house with a basket and a note instructing her to keep him busy. She then invited her guests to take a walk.

The original entrance to the cavern was on the Saunders's land, concealed by a false façade of fallen rocks with a small opening in the furthest corner. Carrying lanterns, they walked down the narrow dirt pathway that wound downward in place of the simple set of steps in the future.

"Does the coven still have this place in your time?" asked Muriel.

"Yes!" replied Jessie, stopping to pop a small pebble out of her shoe. "At some point, my family came into possession of the land, and a house was erected over it to prevent anyone from accidentally finding it. It has been added to a great deal over the years, and now I maintain it as an inn for visitors, but it is set up where it will never pass out of our family."

"And what do you do, Parker?"

"Me? I—um—I am not sure how to explain what I do."

Cassie patted him on the back. "He collects items holding dark magic and brings them back here."

Muriel stopped suddenly and turned to face him. "Dark items?"

"Yes! There are plenty of people who aspire to their own selfish desires and will do anything to accomplish those goals. They find ways to enchant items, call forth demons, and spread their toxic venom," explained Parker. "I just try to make it a little less easy for them."

"That is a very noble profession," Muriel acknowledged. "And you bring them here, you say?"

"Yes! I discovered purely by accident the cave somehow neutralizes the powers and draws the darkness right out of it. It is a pretty amazing thing to witness."

"Now that you mention it, I suppose the natural salt *would* purify the energy, and the sheer amount in the cave would absorb a great deal of the negativity," she muttered to herself. "It makes perfect sense. The fact you discovered it on your own is extremely impressive."

"There's something I don't understand," chimed in Cassie. "How is it that there is plenty of bad magic in our world, but very little good?"

Cassie's inquisitive nature made Muriel smile. "That should be easy enough to figure out. Walking the path of light and goodness requires sacrifice and diligence while expecting nothing in return other than the knowledge that you have done a service to the Mother goddess. Giving in to selfish wants and desires is easy, and it feels good to receive instant gratification. There is an undeniable draw there and most do not have the fortitude to resist. First and foremost, it is a personal choice each individual must make."

"But how?"

"It's all about the intent," replied Muriel as the mouth of the cave opened up. "The power lies in what the heart wants and as soon as your heart and mind are perfectly aligned, there is nothing a person cannot accomplish."

Cassie, Jessie, and Parker found themselves standing before two women, one well into her eighties and one somewhere in her forties. The cave was different than it was in their time, the salt at least three inches thicker beneath their feet. Candles were lit in carved-out spaces in the walls, emitting a cozy soft, warm orange glow, matched only by the hospitable hands extended in greeting.

"Is this the one?" asked the older of the ladies, rushing forward to Jessie, an endearing expression on her face. Muriel nodded and the woman took Jessie's face in her hands. "I am Evita, and I am so pleased to meet you!"

"Oh, my goodness!" Jessie embraced the older woman and pressed her cheek to hers. "I have heard about you my entire life and, never did I imagine in my wildest dreams, I would get the chance to meet you."

Evita pulled a few strands of her hair free and marveled at the bright-blond color. "My dear, you are the most beautiful creature I have ever seen!" Turning, she added, "Look Muriel, my descendants have golden hair! How do you like that?"

"Well, with a little help from a bottle," Jessie chuckled. "My hairdresser certainly has the magic touch!"

The other woman stepped forward, all of four-feet-five, and looked up at Parker, towering over her at well over six feet tall. "Well, you are a giant of a man, aren't you? Are all of the menfolk in our family as big and handsome as you are now?"

Parker smiled down at her, feeling an instant connection to the woman. "I take it you are my Great-Granny Janey?"

"That I am, boy, and it's nice to see the good looks in the family carried on!"

He reached down and took her into a hug, picking her feet up off the ground. Great-Granny Janey laughed and squealed with delight.

"I take it they knew we were coming?" Cassie whispered to Muriel.

"What good is being part of a coven if you can't use your powers to spread the gossip a little faster?" She grinned. "I thought it best I break it to them gently and give them some time to sit with it before I brought you all here."

"They seem to be taking the fact that a bunch of strangers from over four hundred years in the future just dropped out of the sky remarkably well."

Muriel shrugged. "The night before last we were imprisoning the spirit of the daughter of the Devil himself. To be honest, they were thrilled to find out they had grandchildren who were paying them a visit."

After introductions and many questions from both sides, the group gathered around a large stone table to discuss the issue at hand.

"I don't understand why the knowledge was lost in the first place," exclaimed Evita. "How could this possibly happen? We are all so vigilant about teaching our daughters and passing it along."

Cassie rested her chin in her palm. "Things are just very different in our time."

"And the coven gradually fell apart," added Jessie, comfortingly rubbing her friend on the back. "Cassie didn't know we even existed until a couple of days ago. Only three family members descended from the coven were left in the town."

Parker laid his hand over on Cassie's. "One of which sacrificed herself to give us the time we needed to get here."

"What you need is the complete knowledge of the coven," fussed Janey, "but that will involve years of training and gathering other members to teach it to you. There just isn't enough time to do it all."

Evita and Janey looked to Muriel who was staring at a clearly burdened Cassie.

"None of it matters now. All we need to know is that we must come up with something that will work, and we do not have the luxury of time on our side. I will have to be the one to cast the spell to send them back, which means they will have to return before we form the final circle."

Sadie stood up. "So, we come up with one good plan and teach them everything they need to know to carry it out. If they don't survive putting Selena to rest, there won't be any need to learn any new knowledge anyway."

"She is exactly right," Jessie agreed, offering an encouraging smile to her new friend. "Survival comes first. We will figure out the rest later."

After an hour of tossing ideas around and then eliminating them, the group began to grow frustrated with their lack of progress.

"Perhaps we need a wee break," suggested Janey as she stood up, crossed the cave, and returned with a jug of ale, "and a little something to relieve our thirst." Removing the cork, she had a splash before handing it to Parker.

"Tell me," Evita said to Jessie, "Do you have a husband and children?"

"No, but I have an inn," she offered, "directly over top of this place as a matter of fact. If my calculations are right, the original construction, which will be someone's house, should be beginning very soon."

"A home someone builds now that still stands after all that time? That sounds quite exciting."

"The Witch's Globe is a well-loved part of our history," said Parker.

"You named it The Witch's Globe? How clever!" Janey grinned. "No one would ever think to look for a witch in a place named after something to keep one away."

"The tourists like the idea of it," Jessie chuckled, "and I like the idea of taking their money for the experience."

"Don't let her fool you!" Parker chimed in. "That inn is just a reason for her to cook more food than one person could possibly ever eat."

"You enjoy cooking?" asked Evita. "How does someone enjoy so much work?"

"It's not work in our time. We have things called ovens, microwaves, and all sorts of other gadgets that make it easier. I can completely bake a piece of meat in an hour, without a fire, and even boiling water takes only a few moments."

"What about your chores like bringing up water from the river and washing clothes?"

"A pipe brings water straight into your house and all of your laundry can be washed and dried in a couple of hours," replied Parker. "It's no trouble at all."

"How do you know so much about those things?" asked Janey. "That isn't man's work."

He grinned. "Men do their own laundry and cooking in the future. They don't expect the women to do it all."

"Well, the good ones don't anyway!" Jessie laughed.

"Surely THAT is good witchcraft at work," Muriel joked.

Cassie remained quiet and lost in her thoughts, her mind still working on the problem at hand.

Muriel watched her closely. The poor woman had no faith in herself and that was hindering her magic. Perhaps, the time had come to offer a little nudge in the right direction, in the way of planting some new ideas. Turning her head to cough, she muttered a few words under her breath. The corners of her lips twitched up when she saw how quickly her spell took effect.

Suddenly, Cassie's head snapped up. "A witch's globe!" The room went silent as they all turned to stare at her. "Refresh my memory. Aren't they designed to repel witches?"

"Evil witches—yes," replied Muriel, "but good witches can harness their power to scry for visions. Of course, they are fashioned in two different ways for each purpose. Water is used in the glass for divination, but quicksilver is infused with the glass when it is used for warding. Why do you ask?"

"The theory being the quicksilver confuses the witch and muddles their mind, so they become entrapped, right?" The wheels in Cassie's mind were spinning. "Would something like that work on someone as powerful as Selena?"

Muriel cocked her head to one side and pondered the question. "It might, for a very short while, but if she has grown as strong as you have told me, it would only keep her occupied for a tiny bit. It wouldn't hold her permanently."

"She doesn't necessarily need to be held so much as she needs to be rendered powerless," muttered Cassie, her eyes sweeping the cave overhead. "What was that

Parker about the salt in this cave being able to neutralize evil?"

"It has worked in the past—I mean the future—but only on items used in the occult and it has never been tried on a person."

"But it IS stronger in this time," noted Jessie, following Cassie's line of thought. "You said it yourself, Muriel, the righteous acts of the coven have charged this stuff up with good magic, but over time, it has discharged because no one has been practicing in it the way they do now."

"But, what if," Cassie stood, resting her hands flat on the table, "the coven cast a spell infusing the strength of your magic now into the salt and sent it with us when we went back? If she is buried in it, in theory, each time she uses her magic to try and escape, it would be absorbed and neutralized."

A slow smile spread across Muriel's face. "Meaning she would lose power over time as opposed to gaining it. Cassie, that is a brilliant idea!"

"But will it work?"

"I believe it just might!" Muriel went over and took her hands. "The coven has already planned to meet tonight and, given after midnight it is a full moon falling on Samhain, our power will be stronger than it has been in over a hundred years. The timing has never been more perfect. Now, we have much to do! Jessie, you go home with Evita, and Parker, you with your Granny. Spend the afternoon learning all you can from the best while you have the opportunity. Sadie, I need you to pay a visit to the riverbank and bring me a sack full of sand."

"Yes, Mother!"

"Sand?" questioned Cassie.

"We will forge a globe of our own making tonight using our combined magic. It will serve to reinforce our intentions and give you an added layer of protection. We will gather here while the rest of the village slumbers and make our preparations. Now, everyone off, so I can teach Cassie a few of my own tricks."

Once they were alone, Muriel led her over to the altar where the coven's grimoire was kept. Not as thick and worn, Cassie ran her fingers across the newly tanned leather and marveled at the book once more.

"It's quite something to see it as it is now and how it will be to come," she remarked.

Muriel smiled and rested her hands on her shoulders. "I think I prefer your version. I could feel the amount of pure love poured into it as I read through it last night. A great many extraordinary women spent their lives protecting and cherishing the words within."

"You felt it?" Cassie turned and regarded her. "The way I feel things?"

"Probably not quite the same." Muriel picked up the book and brought it over to a table so they could sit. "But, then again, I have a little more experience with the craft than you do. When I hold onto something like this, I don't get visions. Instead, I become a part of its life flow."

"I don't understand." Cassie sat down next to her.

"Everything in this world is a part of something else and all of it is connected. If I pick up a leaf, for instance, I don't just see the tree it fell from directly in front of me, I behold the ground from which the acorn sprouted into the mighty oak. I feel the rain that beat down upon it when the storm came in. I watch as the mother squirrel ran across it to return to her nest to check on her babies. I step into the scene playing out, become a part of it, and experience it all."

"That sounds—overwhelming!" Cassie exhaled sharply. "How do you keep it from driving you insane?"

"Why would it? That leaf is as much a part of this world as I am and when you accept that you are but a small fragment of this grand design while understanding you have been placed as a guardian of it, you find a peace unlike anything you have ever experienced. It is the same way with magic. When you accept who you are and what you are born to be, you flow with the tide instead of battling against it, and you will come to see the world in a different light. At that very moment, the Mother goddess will reveal the secrets of the universe to you."

"Okay, that just made my head hurt."

Muriel laughed and touched her arm. "Perhaps, we should begin with a few baby steps since you are new to all of this."

"How long have you practiced?"

"Since before I was brought into this world!" Seeing the baffled expression on Cassie's face, she elaborated. "I was conceived during a ceremony to bring forth a powerful witch to help others of our kind during difficult times. The seers during my mother's life had begun to see a future where magic was in danger and women of our bloodline would be hunted and slaughtered. Realizing the great need for one to help protect the knowledge and our sisters, they performed a special ritual known only to a precious few to bring forth one with the wisdom of all those who had gone before. I suppose you can say I was born to this role."

"Wow! That's—wow! I would love to know more about that."

"If there is time!" Muriel turned her attention to the book. "Right now, let's concentrate on keeping you alive when you return home, otherwise, you will learn our history in the afterlife."

Taking an apple from the table, she held it up. "I want you to make this hover in the air."

Cassie burst into laughter. "Yeah, okay!"

"Take it in hand and tap into its flow. Don't just see the apple, feel the roots of the tree, hear the chirp of the birds as it formed, taste the rain that helped it to thrive."

Closing her eyes, Cassie wrapped her hands around it and concentrated. Encouraged when she saw a vision in her head of the orchard, she outstretched her fingers and willed it to fly. Popping open one eye, she asked. "Did it work?"

"No! Try again!"

"I can't do it!" Cassie exclaimed, frustrated, after an hour. "It's not in me!"

"It is in you! You just need to dig a little deeper to find it. Perhaps we should move onto something else since time is running short. Spell casting is one of the easiest things to learn and will be the most beneficial in the battle ahead."

Muriel spent the next few hours filling Cassie's head with as much information as possible, teaching her the secrets to formulating spells and how to bring them to life. Though it was a rough go at first, by the end of the day, Cassie had mastered at least one skill.

As the sun began to set, Cassie and Muriel chatted while making their way home.

"What exactly does the coven do during these meetings? I mean do you trade recipes while cursing men who have cheated on their wives?"

Muriel burst into laughter. "Well, we do trade recipes and we have set the occasional stray man back on the straight and narrow, but it's much more than that. We make healing salves for wounds, we cast spells for a good harvest, we pray to the Mother for peace for those who are suffering—and we do tend to drink quite a bit as well."

"I don't know where I fit into this whole picture. Here I am supposedly descended from the ultimate witch, and I can't even make an apple move. Given the past few days, I am not even sure I can trust my own decisions anymore."

"You begin by regaining confidence in yourself. Just because you chose poorly once, doesn't mean you will again. We all make mistakes, but as long as we learn from them, they aren't mistakes—only lessons."

"I guess that's one way to look at it."

"Parker seems like a good man," Muriel's eyes cut to Cassie, a sly smirk on her face, "and he is quite handsome, as well."

"I suppose."

"Does he have a wife and children?"

"No, and I am fairly certain he doesn't want them, either."

"Don't be silly," Muriel waved her remark off. "All men want a woman to warm their bed and children to carry on their name. I am sure he is no different."

"It's not as important in the future."

"What about you? Do you wish to marry and have children?"

"I have never given it much thought. My job has always been my primary focus." Cassie's shoulders slouched a bit. "Besides, I have lousy taste in men."

"You might want to consider it, after all, you are the last of our line and it would be a shame for our family to end with you."

"It is bad enough when my mother points out my ticking biological clock, but to have my ancestor, the head of a witch coven, bring it up raises it to a whole new level. No pressure there!"

"It is something to think about."

"Finding the right person isn't so easy with six billion people in the world."

Muriel stopped. "How many is a billion?"

"A million times a thousand."

"How many is a million?"

Cassie's eyes rolled back as she thought. "A thousand thousands, I think?"

"That is a great many people! How is there room for all of them?"

"The world is a bigger place than you know. Now you understand why it is so hard to find the right person."

"Oh, I don't know." Muriel took her by the arm. "Sometimes what you are searching all over the world for turns out to have been right in front of you all along."

Jessie and Parker were already at Muriel's home when they arrived. The family enjoyed another fine meal together later that night. Muriel and Thurston turned in early. The elder witch came to get them from the barn a little before midnight.

"Won't your husband miss you?" asked Cassie as they lit a few lanterns.

"Oh no! I slipped some valerian into his drink. He will be out cold until morning."

"You sure do drug that man a great deal," mumbled Parker. "I hope you don't do any permanent damage to him."

"It is for his own good. The less he knows, the better off he is," she retorted with a chuckle.

The cave was illuminated with over a hundred candles. Tables of food and drink lined the walls and black hooded figures danced together in a circle.

Cassie stopped to take in the scene, a welcoming feeling of loving warmth washing over her and filling her with happiness. A tear formed in the corner of her eye when she realized this would be the last night they would all be together, for tomorrow the thirteen would sacrifice their lives to save the coven and the three of them would be returned home to deal with the aftermath. Stepping away, her attention was drawn to a painting resting on a makeshift shelf. It was of a younger woman and an older man, who looked oddly familiar, but she couldn't place from where.

"Ah, I see you admiring the portrait. That painting came with us here and has been in my family for generations. I am to assume it did not remain with us?"

"No, unfortunately. Who are they?"

Muriel smiled. "That is the King of the Fae and that is his daughter, the Mother Goddess, Danu."

"The Fae? The old gods? You worship them?"

Muriel reached out and straightened it. "We serve them, for they are the true guardians of the world."

"He looks so stinking familiar to me for some reason!" Cassie racked her brain.

"They say the Fae King will appear when you least expect it, either to lend a helping hand or to have a good laugh at your expense given his mischievous nature. To be in his favor is a great gift, but to be on his bad side makes for a miserable experience. It is said that the portrait is a gift from him directly."

"Really? How did that come about?"

"The story goes that many years ago, on an island far away from here, the old ones were served by a race of beautiful women, chosen and raised from a young age to that purpose. They were protected and concealed from the outside world by the gods and lived happily with their sisters. One day, a ship caught in a terrible storm crashed onto the rocks. There was only one survivor, the handsome captain, who washed up on their shores. Cairstine, the leader of the group at the time, took pity on him and brought him under their protection. It took weeks for him to recover and by the time he did, the two had fallen deeply in love. Knowing their union would be forbidden, but desperate to be with her captain, she prayed to the goddess, Danu, for assistance. Ever the romantic herself, the goddess appeared and was merciful after hearing their plight, agreeing to appeal to her father on the young couple's behalf. Never being able to deny a heartfelt request from his daughter, the King of the Fae granted them his blessing and gave them this painting as a reminder of his merciful gift as they began their life on a new shore far away."

"That is quite the romantic story." Cassie brushed away an errant tear as her eyes swept the room. "Everything about this life—the love, the people, the sisterhood—it is all truly a beautiful gift."

"Don't be sad," Muriel whispered in her ear. "This night is a celebration of the Mother goddess, Danu, the women we are and are yet to be, and the goodness we have set forth into the world. I am beyond proud to know you will be my legacy in it."

"That's a lot to live up to. I am not sure I'm up for the job."

"My dear, you come from an ancient line of the most powerful women in the world," she sighed, "but the problem is you never knew it. I think it's time that issue was rectified. I have been giving it a great deal of consideration, and I believe there may be another way to give you the confidence you need to defeat Selena."

"What do you mean?"

Muriel took her by the hand and led her into a small, empty chamber off to the side where it was quiet. "You have the power to hold an artifact and see its history. I think I am old enough to be considered a 'relic'. Take my hands in yours and read me."

"I don't know. I've never tried it with a person," she said with hesitation, her voice full of doubt.

Lifting her eyebrows, Muriel uniquely offered a bit of encouragement to drive home her point. "Think of all the trouble you would have saved yourself if you had forced yourself to read Thomas and Bethany all those years ago."

"WOW! That was kind of harsh, don't you think?"

Muriel held out her hands and wiggled her fingers. "Sometimes, the truth hurts, my dear, and the most well-learned lessons are the painful ones. Now, quit dithering and do as I say!"

Taken back a bit by the 'tough love' approach, Cassie blew out a hard breath, took the coven leader's hands in her own, and closed her eyes. Allowing the vision to wash over her, Cassie was expelled from her body, taken on a journey through time, and shown the images and stories of a thousand women who had come before, all filled with love, strength, and the sacred knowledge of the coven. She watched their lives play out in great detail, marveling at all they had accomplished with what nature had to offer, leaving her dumbstruck by the many revelations laid out before her.

When the flow of wisdom slowed and broke a mere few moments later, she fell backward to the ground, her body trembling from the intensity of all she saw and felt, a raging wake cascading throughout every cell in her body. Closing her eyes, Cassie lay still until she was able to regain her senses. She heard Muriel call out for Parker and ask him to hold her hand, and when she came around, Parker was staring back at her.

"Hey! Are you okay?" he asked, brushing the hair from her forehead, his face filled with worry.

"I think so?" She tried to sit up, but still shaky, she fell backward again. He caught her and slipped his arm around her waist to steady her. As they touched, another startling vision was revealed.

"Just take it easy. I've got you and I am not going to let you go," she heard him say, but it wasn't from the Parker who sat with her. Cassie found herself able to see beyond his Earthly form, straight into his soul, and it was one she found extremely familiar on many levels. It was then she understood the meaning—the two had lived lives together before and they had always found their way back to each other, possessing an enduring love, one that time, nor death, could separate. Their lips naturally drew together once more, and their kiss burned with an intensity neither had ever experienced in any lifetime. They pulled back and stared into each other's eyes, but the spell broke when they heard Muriel call the coven to order from the center of the circle.

"I don't know what the hell that was but promise me we will pick it up later when we are alone?" he whispered, still at a loss as to what they had just experienced.

"Uh-huh!" she managed as he helped her to her feet and escorted her into the main chamber.

Muriel's eyes found hers, and the elder woman offered a wink with her all-knowing smile.

With her newfound knowledge, Cassie came to a staggering realization—the coven leader knew a great deal more about the mysteries of the universe than she had let on and was far more powerful than anyone would ever understand.

"Sisters! You know why we have gathered. The ones who will come after us need our help and we will always offer guidance and protection to our own. Join me and share your power to help save those yet to be born." She poured the bag of sand at her feet and kneeled. Extending her hands, she raised the grains above her head with her magic and spun them into a large ring, making a shape without touching them. A ball started to form. Janey came forward next, flicking her hands as if adding a dash of something to the mix. Constance and Sadie went next, smiling at their mother as they each added two handfuls of salt from the cave floor and began working their fingers in the same manner. As each coven member came to the front, Cassie, Jessie, and Parker watched with amazement as the sand slowly morphed into glass and rose into the air, high into the roof of the cave, emitting a brilliant bright light from its core. Evita would be the one to add the last ingredient adding an incantation to strengthen the power. She removed the stopper from a bottle and used her abilities to raise the quicksilver into the air to join with the glass. When it was completed, the witch's globe turned white and a silvery mixture flowed through it, moving like a lava lamp. Muriel caught it as it dropped, corked the small opening, and placed it in a wooden box filled with the energized salt before presenting it to Cassie. "When she is contained, it will turn black, but once her power has completely waned, it will turn this color again. You must not open it under any circumstances once she is sealed in until it is as it is now."

"Thank you," she said gratefully, accepting the precious gift, and turning to the others. "Thank you all and know, we will do our best to make you proud."

Muriel smiled and touched her on the arm, happy to see Cassie so accepting of who she was. "Now! For the original thirteen of us, this is our last night in this world. Tonight, we celebrate the love we have been blessed with in this life. Eat! Drink! Commemorate our final Samhain with us as we prepare to join our ancestors, moving into our new positions as your guardians, a role we look forward to accepting."

The lively sound of music began to play as the women clapped and embraced each other. The rest of the night was surprisingly light-hearted and full of joy.

Cassie was downing a cup of ale, trying to clear her head, when Muriel came over to join her. "Did you get your fill of our family in your vision?"

"That was an experience I think is going to take me years, and several well-paid therapists, to process," she confessed, "but it is good to know I have so many wonderful women in my corner, watching my back."

"Indeed you do, and you always will, especially when you need it the most. Never forget who you are and where you come from, even if you were a little late in discovering it."

Cassie could feel Parker watching her intently from across the room. "*That* was a bit of a surprise, as well."

Muriel turned, raised her cup in his direction, and smirked. "Not to me. You don't need to be a witch to see you two were meant to find each other." Her eyes drifted to Jessie and Sadie who were in a quiet corner, standing close to each other, talking. "Just as you do not need to be gifted to see *those* two were destined for each other, as well."

Cassie followed her gaze and gasped, nearly choking on her ale. "Jessie and Sadie?" she sputtered and coughed, wiping the ale from her chin.

"Yes, of course!" Muriel looked at her peculiarly. "Why are you so surprised? Are women falling in love with each other still taboo?"

"No, not at all—I just didn't realize Jessie swung that way."

Muriel scrunched up her face. "Well, I don't know what a 'swing' has to do with it, but I know one thing for certain—two halves of one soul will always seek each other out. When they are able to find one another, it is a true gift—the form it masks itself in simply isn't important. It is just a shame they will have such little time together."

"Hi!" Parker said awkwardly, having worked his way over to them.

"Parker? Is Jessie a lesbian?"

"Yes, of course, she is! Didn't you know?"

"No! Apparently, I'm missing a lot these days!"

Muriel patted her on the shoulder. "Don't worry, you will catch up. If you will excuse me, there are quite a few people I wish to bid farewell to," her eyes drifted to Parker, "and I think you two have some things to discuss."

"Are we going to talk about that kiss?" whispered Parker as soon as Muriel stepped away.

"Not right now," she replied, pointing to Janey who was making her way over to them. "I think you should spend some more time with Granny Janey, while you can!"

He handed her his cup. "I believe I will. I've grown quite fond of that little lady!"

Parker laughed as Janey took him by the arm and pulled him into the dancing circle. They were soon joined by Jessie and Sadie, as Constance pulled Cassie in, as well. The three thoroughly enjoyed their night of revelry as Muriel and Evita watched over the group from afar.

"Are we giving them enough to go up against Selena?" asked Evita.

Muriel sighed heavily. "They have the tools, but the real question is whether or not they believe in themselves enough to do this. If there is any doubt, Selena will cut them down and wipe what's left of our coven from the Earth." Turning, she placed her arm around her old friend. "We can only pray to the old ones and ask them to aid their plight while hoping what we have done is enough." Looking at the portrait, she added, "Perhaps, I will put in a special offering and an extra prayer to Finn, the Fae King, just for good measure."

Cassie needed a moment to herself. The past few days had been a whirlwind and she was having a hard time wrapping her head around it all. Something within her had changed, and she found herself yearning for the type of magical life she never knew existed. Deciding it was time for some fresh air, she headed outside, taking a seat at the base of an ancient oak tree illuminated by the soft light of the full moon. Leaning against it, she felt something she had never felt before—the energy of the Earth flowing through its bark. It was a connection she had heard poets speak of, but never felt for herself until that very night. Closing her eyes, she allowed the force to join with hers, sending tiny vibrations humming throughout her bloodstream into every cell in her being. Her body became more relaxed and comfortable with each beat.

"A penny for your thoughts," she heard Parker say.

"That might add up to be quite the bill," she teased, smiling with her eyes still closed, unwilling to break from the welcoming warmth that engulfed her. "I have more thoughts than I ever thought possible."

"I have never been a rich man, so why start now? Some things are worth the price." He waved his hand. "Do you mind if I join you, or would you prefer to be alone?"

"Please!" She stuck out her hand and patted the ground next to her.

"Maybe we could talk about that thing that happened earlier?" he suggested guardedly as he sat down and raised his knees to his chest.

"I don't think that is necessary."

"Oh!" Parker's voice was full of disappointment. "I was hoping…"

She raised and cut him off. "Because there is nothing to talk about."

"I see!" he muttered, scratching the side of his face.

"Yeah, so do I!" Cassie slipped her hand over and cupped his chin. "I have never seen anything more clearly in my life."

Her lips went to his, taking him off guard. He reacted quickly and didn't give her the chance to change her mind. Drawing her into an ardent kiss, he wound his arms around her and pulled her body close to his.

"I don't know what tomorrow holds," he managed, "but, if this is the end, there is nowhere else I would rather spend my last night in this world than with you. I don't know how or when it happened, but I have fallen hopelessly in love with you."

Cassie took his hand and pressed it to her cheek. "If this is our last time in this lifetime together, know I will find you in the next, no matter what! We are meant to be together—always."

She slid onto his lap, straddling him as she wrapped one arm around his neck while using her free hand to lift her skirt. Filled with desire, the amorous couple wasted no time removing each other's clothing, tossing them aside until they were naked and rolling with each other on the forest floor. Beneath the full moon, they joined in a primal mating ritual, finishing with an explosion that left them each speechless, out of breath, and completely sated.

"Wow!" they said in unison before bursting into a bout of laughter. Nestled in the crook of his arm, Cassie smiled.

Parker looked down. "Not that I'm complaining in the least, but I feel like our first time together should have been more 'wine and roses' and less 'mud and twigs'," he said and plucked a leaf off her thigh.

"I think this was pretty perfect," she confessed, snuggling in closer. "If we had tried this in our time, we would have probably ended up in jail for indecent exposure."

"Good point," he conceded.

"Besides, I wouldn't trade this view of the stars for anything."

The group returned before dawn and slept in a bit, leaving Muriel and Thurston alone for, what he was unaware, would be their last breakfast together. Muriel spent the rest of the day watching Thurston perform his household chores, committing every detail to memory.

Constance and Sadie helped the three pack, loading up bags with all the items from their time that might come in handy and giving them some final tips on how to use them.

Supper was a lively affair.

Muriel wanted to ensure Thurston and her girls had a
good memory to keep with them, so they feasted and
sang the evening away. Well before midnight, as they
were preparing to leave, Evita appeared outside,
tapping on the window.

"Muriel! Something is wrong! You must come!
Selena is breaking through."

They gathered their things and followed Evita to the
circle in the woods not far from where they were, and
watched as the ground trembled and cracks began to
form. An unearthly cackle rose from beneath their
feet. The others had already taken hemlock, as well as
their appointed places, leaving only Janey, Evita, and
Muriel to finish the circle.

"There is no more time!" Muriel proclaimed over the
roar of the wind that had picked up as if a huge storm
were about to bear down on them at any moment.

"Take your vials and your places, sisters, and know,
you do this to save the future! We will greet each
other on the other side."

Muriel turned to Cassie and grasped her hands. "I
wish I had more time. There is so much I want you to
learn. Above all, my dear, you must remember to

believe in yourself and promise me you will learn all you can to carry on our family's legacy!"

"I will do my best," she vowed, "but I don't know how I am going to be able to without you!"

"If only there was some other way to be sure," Muriel fretted, "I don't want our kind to disappear into nothingness, only to be forgotten by the ages."

"I could go with them!" Sadie suddenly offered, rushing to her mother's side. "You have taught me everything you know, and I can teach them. I know I don't have the bloodline, but I do have the knowledge. Perhaps, it was the reason you and my father were brought together all along."

"Mother! That's the answer we have been searching for!" Constance came forward. "Who better to teach it than someone who learned directly from the best? Sadie knows all we do, and she could be exactly the tutor they need in their time, while Miles and I carry on the line from here."

Muriel touched both her daughter's faces and a sly grin crossed her lips. "Oh, my sweet, smart girls! What a perfect idea!" she praised while discreetly winking at Cassie, letting her know it had been her plan all along. "It gives me great comfort to know the two of you will always be watching over our kind now and in the future. But there is one final thing that must be done. The coven must have a new leader and there can be no question!" The ground rocked once more, sending them all stumbling, nearly falling to their knees. Pulling a dagger from her belt, Muriel dragged the blade across her palm, slicing open her hand, and did the same to Cassie's, clasping the open gashes together. "By the blood of my blood, I give to you, the power of all those who have gone before you and all that comes with it. Accept the gift of your legacy and become the force of nature you were born to be. Blessed be, and remember who you are, Cassie Summers, for you are the leader of the next generation of witches! I trust you to rule them well! I have complete faith in you!"

Evita and Janey made their way over to Jessie and Parker, repeating the ceremony, and passing their own generations of power down to their descendants. The elders said their hasty 'goodbyes' and went to their final resting places. With Muriel being the last piece of the puzzle that needed to be put in place, a bolt of lightning appeared from the sky and struck in the center of the circle as a pair of ghostly fingers began to claw up from the soil.

Muriel quickly kissed Cassie on the cheek and turned, doing the same to Sadie. "Go and be well my girls! I love you both more than you will ever know. I will be watching over you from the other side!" With that, she recited the spell and waved, watching them go with a peaceful expression on her face.

As they were pulled away, Cassie could see her tearfully embrace Constance one final time, drink the vial, and crawl down into the grave, setting the ground still once more. The four landed with a 'thud' in the middle of the circle in the year 2020.

"Those landings don't get any easier, do they?" groaned Parker as he rolled to one side, clutching his ribs, slowly climbing to his feet next to Jessie and Sadie who were helping each other up.

"Complain about your aches and pains later, assuming we survive all this," said Cassie, who had landed gracefully on her feet and slipped two bags off her shoulder, one containing the box, the other the book. "Sadie, I hereby proclaim you the new protector of the coven's sacred and most holy book," she said, unceremoniously tossing it into her arms. "Now, go stuff it in a tree trunk or something."

Sadie caught it with her arms, nodded, and was off.

Removing four rocks from a bag, Parker placed them in different locations on the circle.

"What are you doing?"

"Granny Janey taught me a few things, one of them being how to use these crystals to reform the sacred ring."

Jessie took out a jug and went around to all the skeletons, dousing them with oil. Reciting an incantation as she held out her hands, they all watched as a spark ignited a six-inch-high blue loop around them. "Thank you, Evita!" she said, stepping back to observe the result, pleased with herself.

Cassie looked off towards the horizon as she planted the box in the center, the orange flames from Ilene's house illuminating the sky as the sound of fire engines filled the air. "Take your places. We don't know how long we have." Cassie finished up and the four positioned themselves back-to-back around it, prepared for the battle to come. The atmosphere shifted when a powerful downdraft exploded and a loud high-pitched shrill surrounded them.

"Where is she?" shouted Cassie.

Sadie pointed up toward the treetops. "There!"

"The bitch can fly? Seriously?"

"This bitch can do much more than fly," snapped Selena as she landed just outside the circle. Inhaling sharply, she laughed. "You are the one with the blood of the coven leader and the last of your kind. It seems you are just the person I am looking for."

"Hold your ground," ordered Cassie, "she cannot enter this circle."

Selena pressed her palms to her cheeks and feigned fear. "Oh, how will I ever defeat you?" her voice dripping with sarcasm. Her face hardened and she strode across the line, killing the flame instantly while breaking the seal. "I learned a few things while I was imprisoned. Muriel's old tricks won't work on me anymore."

Cassie glanced nervously over her shoulder at the others who were staring back at her, unsure of what to do next. "RUN! SAVE YOURSELVES!" she shouted to them and planted herself in front of Selena, giving them time to scatter into the nearby woods.

"I suppose I should thank you," Selena taunted as she came closer. "After all, I wouldn't be here without your action that broke the seal—you and that Thomas fellow. You are welcome, by the way. You don't have to worry about him anymore. He won't ever order another woman around."

"What did you do to him?"

Selena stalked around Cassie, circling her prey. "I never was one for having a man tell me what to do, no matter who he might be. I am the daughter of the Dark One, and I will never be at the mercy of another."

"You killed him?"

"I daresay you'll miss him about as much as I will."

Cassie jerked back when Selena reached out and let the back of her hand glide across her cheek, regarding her with keen interest.

"He was too ambitious and had no respect for his elders. Instead of asking what he could do for me, he couldn't stop talking about what he wanted me to do for him. Such a selfish man!" She tsked. "No woman needs to have that kind of misery and grief in her life." Selena twirled around and stopped to look down at one of the skeletons. "Speaking of ones who cause grief, I think it's time this cat stopped playing with the mouse and finally put you out of your misery."

Her eyes narrowed in on Cassie who shouted to the others, "NOW!"

Parker emerged from the center of the woods first, reciting words as he moved. The four stones he laid began to glow and a warm white light flowed between them, erupting into flames nearly six feet high. Jessie and Sadie appeared next, each from one side, holding up their hands, casting a spell as they approached. The bones of the thirteen shook and shifted, each rising as whole skeletons from their Earthly graves, joining hands and forming another perimeter around Selena and Cassie.

"You think your circle of fire and bones is going to hold me for long?" she spat to Cassie.

"No, I don't think it will, but I only needed to keep you talking and have it hold you for a few minutes."

"And after that?" scoffed Selena. "The only thing strong enough to stop me was my grimoire and since it is now a part of me, you are out of options."

"Oh, I am sure I have a trick or two still up my sleeve. After all, I am the direct descendant of the greatest witch to ever live." Cassie stepped aside to reveal the wooden box.

Selena looked down—and burst into laughter. "A wooden box? You have *got* to be joking?" Drawing back her hand, she struck Cassie hard across the face with such a stunning amount of force that she flew through the air and landed several feet away. Walking over to the container, Selena flicked her hand and used her magic to rip off the lid. Curious as to what they thought could hold her, she looked inside. Her head inclined to one side as she slowly fell to her knees, her eyes fixated on the silvery flow within the globe, inexplicably unable to break her gaze. "What— is—this?"

Cassie rolled to one side, clutching her ribs, crawled over to look her in the eye, and whispered, "Gotcha!" as she yanked off the cork. Clambering to her feet, she wiped the blood from her cheek, lifted her arms, and commanded, "I call upon those who have gone before to lend me your wisdom and strength, and stand with me this sacred night to put an end to this darkness once and for all."

The flames went out and the skeletons collapsed in a heap—only to be replaced with the luminous spirits of the coven from all the centuries before. The brilliant golden light emitting from the ghosts of a thousand women holding hands appeared, bathing the area in radiance, surrounding Cassie as Parker, Jessie, and Sadie joined her. The wind rose once more, and an ancient chant from days long gone filled the air being produced by the spirits around Selena. Though she struggled to free herself, cursing the beings of light come to banish her, she was trapped, unable to break her gaze, leaving her powerless to fight back against the legion of those who had gone before. As the words grew louder, Selena's solid appearance began to splinter into smaller pieces before finally shattering into shards that were no bigger than grains of rice.

The collective group pursed their lips and blew upon the breeze until it was strong enough to lift the particles and push them into the globe. Once inside, Cassie picked it up, stuffed in the cork, and sealed it once and for all with a spell she had learned from Muriel, the silver already overtaking the black in a spinning whirlwind inside. When the deed was complete, the heaviness that had permeated the area immediately lifted and was replaced with a loving warmth and light, unlike anything she had ever experienced before. The family she never knew she had brought tears of joy to her eyes.

"Thank you all!" said Cassie. "I will do my best to make you proud and to carry on the family legacy. I will not let you or your astounding lives ever be forgotten. You have my word!"

One by one, each spirit slowly dissipated until only one remained—Muriel.

"Well done, my darlings," she said with a smile as bright as the full moon on that auspicious Halloween night. "Blessed be, and know we are always here for you. You need only to call!"

With that, she vanished leaving the four alone in the darkness.

Once the noise grew silent and the dead had settled once more, the group looked around at each other, seemingly lost.

"I don't suppose there is a car nearby?" asked Jessie, out of the blue.

"Nope!" replied Cassie as she looked around. "Looks like we are hoofing it from here."

"What's a car?" questioned Sadie.

Slowly making their way up the street, they arrived back at the inn a little over an hour later, exhausted and at a loss for words. Jessie was the last one through the doorway and kicked it closed behind her. Still on edge, when the doorbell rang, they all tensed and exchanged wary glances. Parker went to it and slowly inched open the door, peeking through the crack.

"TRICK OR TREAT!" shouted a group of children.

"Oh shit! I forgot that it's Halloween," he muttered.

Dragging her feet, Jessie picked up a bowl of candy from the nearby table and shoved the whole thing into the first child's arms. Leaning down, she whispered, "Share this with your friends and spread the word— The Witch's Globe is all out of candy and if anyone throws toilet tissue in my trees, they will wake up with a bed full of toads. Believe me when I say I can make that happen! Got it?"

The terrified little boy dressed as a clown nodded vigorously and ran away from the house as fast as he could, spilling candy as he went. The other children ran after him, shouting and demanding their cut of the loot.

"Did you say, 'thank you'?" called his mother from the sidewalk.

Jessie offered a one-finger salute and slammed the door shut before turning off the outside light and rejoining the others.

"What's Halloween and what was that thing called candy you gave them?" asked Sadie.

Cassie lowered her head and giggled. "Oh Sadie, you have so much to learn!"

9

CHAPTER NINE

"What do you mean he isn't answering his phone? Our baby is coming tonight!" She had been in labor for the better part of the day, but the pain was only now becoming unbearable.

"I am sorry, Bethany," said Renee, their housekeeper, "I have tried every number he gave me several times, but it just goes to voicemail."

"It's alright," assured Helen, the midwife as she helped her into a gown. "We are here, and we will get you through this. Dr. Armstrong has already done his part anyway."

Another strong contraction hit her, causing her to double over and scream out in pain. They were coming faster with little time between each one. "Maybe we should go to the hospital. They have drugs there for this."

"It's too late for that. This child will be entering the world sooner than you know. Furthermore, Dr. Armstrong insisted on a homebirth," reminded Helen, helping her over to the birthing chair. "He wanted to make sure everything went well and that you were comfortable in your quarters."

"Yeah, well he is not the one having this baby, and besides he's not even here."

"We are better equipped than the hospital and we have everything we need. He spared no expense."

"Everything except drugs," muttered Bethany as she settled in, crying out once more, the pressure becoming more intense by the moment.

"Let's have a look," said Helen, placing her feet in the stirrups. "Oh! The baby is crowning! I am going to need you to push extra hard on the next contraction!"

"Thomas should be here!" she shouted, the birth now advancing quickly.

"Well, he's not!" snapped Renee, taking her hand. "He will just be surprised when he finally does get home. Now, PUSH!"

Bethany bore down hard and within minutes, a new life had arrived in the world.

"It's a girl!" announced Helen, wrapping her in a blanket before handing her to her mother.

"A girl!" Bethany whispered, carefully cradling her in her arms, tears of joy streaming down her face. "Thomas will be so happy. After years of trying, we finally have our miracle baby."

"Let me have her for just a minute," said Renee. The woman took the newborn to carefully clean up, regarding her with excitement, as Helen tended to her patient. Glancing at her watch, she noted, "Well, would you look at that? Baby Armstrong was born at 11:59 on October 31st. I guess she wanted to be a Samhain baby."

"Have you picked out a name?" asked Renee, carefully handing her the baby back.

"We did. Thomas insisted we name her after one of his ancestors, and I wanted my family's name to be included, as well, since I have no one left." She looked down at the dark-haired beauty. "Welcome to the world, Millicent Giles Armstrong. We will call her 'Millie' for short."

Renee hovered protectively over the mother and child. "What a lovely name for an extraordinary little girl!"

Renee and Helen looked at each other, devilish smirks on their faces.

10

CHAPTER TEN

After Ilene's funeral three days later, the group returned to the inn and Jessie hung the 'closed' sign on the door.

"Are you shutting down?" asked Cassie as she slipped off her heels.

"Just for a few weeks." She sat down next to Sadie and laid her head over on her shoulder as she grasped her hand. "I thought I might just take some time to show Sadie how we do things in this time."

"It is a great deal to learn," admitted Sadie, "but I have a wonderful teacher and, so far, I am loving it. The kitchen alone is worth making the trip through time. Do you know how fast I can cook now?"

"You two are perfect for each other!" Parker chuckled, passing around glasses of whisky.

"What about you, Cassie?" asked Jessie. "What are you going to do now?"

"Well," she swished the liquid around in her glass, "I have some promises to keep. I thought I might start by trying to track down some of the descendants of the original coven. I am sure there are others like me who have some abilities they might not understand."

"Actually," Parker sat down next to her, "I was hoping to offer you a job."

"A job?"

"Yes, you see, Selena was not the only bad seed out there, and, as I said before, my team and I have more work than we can handle. We could sure use someone with, not only your 'Head of the Coven' powers, but your remarkable ability to get visions from occult items. It would come in extremely handy."

"That's an excellent idea!" exclaimed Jessie.

"We can even put you on salary," he added, "but you would have to spend most of your time on this side of the pond. Maybe even give up that apartment in California, if you can bear to part with it, that is."

Jessie appeared hopeful. "Even better!"

Cassie sighed. "I have to admit, this little town has kind of grown on me and I do need to be close to

Sadie so she can help me navigate my way around this whole witch thing, plus the book and the salt cave are here…"

"And I know this great place you can stay!" Jessie grinned excitedly. "Not to mention all these wonderful new friends you have made!"

"Well, how can I possibly say 'no' to an offer like that?"

"YAY!" Jessie and Sadie sprung from the sofa and embraced her in an enormous hug as Parker laughed.

"Forget this stuff!" Jessie took her glass and set it aside. "I have some excellent champagne I have been saving for a special occasion. Don't go anywhere while Sadie and I grab it."

As soon as they were alone, Parker got up and went over to Cassie, leaning on the arm of her chair. "Now that is settled, I think it's about time we talked about that night under the tree!"

"What would you like me to say?" she asked, staring straight ahead, sporting a mischievous grin.

"Say you will let me take you out on an actual date after I get back."

Her smile faded. "Get back from where?"

"Tying up loose ends."

"What sort?"

He intertwined his fingers in hers. "For starters, I need to go out to Armstrong's house and make it appear he just up and left. Then, I need to petition for a warrant for his arrest, just to cover ourselves, and make an effort to find him by paying a visit to his home in London."

"Will that be enough?"

Parker pressed his lips to the back of her hand. "Trust me, I have done this hundreds of times. I know what I am doing."

"I should go with you to the cottage."

"No!" he protested. "That's not necessary. You have been through enough. I can handle it alone."

"I want to," she assured. "I *need* to. I think it might help me find some closure."

Parker thought for a moment before finally conceding. "Alright, but just there. I will go to London alone. It will raise too many questions if you accompany me, and we need to make it appear you were just an innocent bystander in all of this."

"Fair enough!"

Jessie and Sadie returned with the bottles and the four spent the rest of the night celebrating life.

The following day, Cassie and Parker drove out to Thomas's house by the water. His truck was parked in the driveway, and they found the front door unlocked. Parker drew his gun and cautiously pushed it open. Checking inside and finding it empty, he holstered his weapon and waved Cassie inside.

"It's weird being back here after all that has happened," remarked Cassie, rubbing the gooseflesh on her arms as she peered around.

"If you want to wait in the car, I won't be long."

"No! I need to be here."

The house was eerily quiet, adding to the overall sinister atmosphere. "This was where she was born."

"Who?" he asked as he went to a desk in the corner.

"Selena. I had a vision the last time I was here of a baby being born and immediately sent away. I didn't know it was her at the time, but now I know better."

Parker looked up from the papers he was sifting through. "What do you suppose she did with him?"

It was then Cassie noticed the clothing and scattered ashes on the floor. "I think I just found him."

He went over to join her and grimaced. "You think that's all that's left of him?"

Cassie pointed to a piece of leather sticking out of the pile. Parker reached down and picked it up by the corner, shaking it off. Flipping open the wallet, their suspicions were confirmed by Thomas's driver's license. "Well, on a brighter note, there is no body to dispose of."

"I almost feel sorry for him," she muttered. "Almost!"

Parker quickly went through it to find several credit cards and a great deal of cash. "I will drop it at a homeless shelter. He has no use for the money and the card trail will make it look like he is still alive and on the run." Finding a picture hidden in one of the slots, he pulled it out and held it up. "Who do you suppose this lovely woman is?"

"What the hell?" she exclaimed as she snatched it from him. "That's a picture of Bethany. Why would he have it in his wallet after all this time?"

"Guilt maybe?"

"I don't know, but it's weird." She frowned. "This is a picture of her I have never seen before."

"What's so strange about that?"

"Well, by the looks of it, it had to have been taken when we were in college, and I just think I would have seen it. Her hair is a bit darker and styled differently here, as well."

"Could be the lighting and maybe it was taken before you two met."

"Yeah, that's probably it."

She handed it back, but Parker refused. "Keep it. I know you must still harbor some ill will for what they did behind your back, but she very well may have been under his spell. At the end of the day, she was like a sister to you, and you should hold on to the good memories."

"You're right." Cassie tucked the picture in her back pocket and watched as Parker took a knife from the kitchen. He went back over to the desk. Using the blade, he pried open a locked drawer. "What are you doing?"

"Making sure there isn't anything here that alludes to you being anyone but a colleague he called in for a consultation," he replied as it popped open. Removing the contents, he carefully went through them before feeling underneath for anything else that may have been hidden.

"Is anything there?"

Parker held up an extremely thick manilla file he found with her name on it. Cassie reached for it, but he held it back. "Whatever is in this no longer matters. Perhaps it is best if you leave it be. I can simply torch it in the fireplace, and we can move on with our lives."

She thought for a moment before taking it from his hands and clutching it to her breast. "How about we just hang onto it without reading it for the time being? I don't think I am ready to see what's in it, but someday, who knows? There may be information about my family in it that I may not be able to locate otherwise."

"Whatever you like, sweetheart."

Parker quickly went over everything else, taking anything that referred to Cassie, or magic, to look at later. Once he was satisfied, he tossed Thomas's clothing in the river, scattered the ashes, and grabbed the keys to the truck, which, along with his cell phone, he tossed in the front seat.

"Why are you doing that?"

"Well, with any luck," he said as he opened his car door for her, "someone will steal the truck and the phone and take it cross-country, leaving the authorities to believe he's in hiding."

"You are pretty good at this!"

"Years of experience," he said as he closed the door.

"Now, I am taking you back to Jessie's place where I want you to stay until I return from London."

"How long will you be?"

"Well, I need to attend to some SB business while I am there, so no more than a couple of days. I am not planning on leaving until the morning." He looked over at her hopefully. "I don't suppose you would like to have a nice romantic dinner with me before I go…and maybe…. talk about that certain spark between us?"

"No, I don't want to talk about it," she replied, turning her face away to conceal her smile.

"Oh!" he said, with obvious disappointment in his voice.

"I think I would rather reignite it than discuss it."

"OH!" Parker's face instantly lit up.

Later that evening, they enjoyed a romantic candlelight dinner, prepared by Jessie and Sadie, under the ivy-covered pergola in the garden of the inn.

Afterward, they came inside to find a trail of flower petals leading up the stairs to the 'Honeymoon Suite' of the inn.

"Looks like Jessie and Sadie went all out," said Parker nervously, gripping her hand tightly. "For the record, I didn't put them up to this. I would never presume—not that I don't want to—I just don't want you to feel pressured—even though we have already—it is technically our first date after all—I mean, technically—even though we already…"

Cassie pressed her finger to his lips to hush his ramblings. "I know you didn't put them up to it because I did. I think some alone time is long overdue."

"Good!" Parker let out the breath he had been holding and grinned. "I think so too."

Taking him by the hand, Cassie pulled him up the stairs, into the room filled with roses and candles, where they took their time, enjoying each other and making love until dawn.

Parker still had a stupid grin on his face, and Cassie's perfume on his shirt, when he arrived in

London the next day. His night with her had been
nothing short of astounding and he couldn't wait to
get back into her arms. After visiting the SB office
and formalizing the warrant for Thomas's arrest, he
dropped the man's wallet in an alley near a large soup
kitchen where a homeless encampment was nearby.
With his loose ties tidied up, only one final stop stood
between him and another glorious night with the
woman he had fallen hopelessly in love with.

He was taken aback a bit by the Armstrong family
home. Given the style and location of the mansion, it
had been the centerpiece of an expensive estate at one
time. The land must have been sold off at some point
because newer homes had sprung up around it.
Though not ramshackle by any stretch of the
imagination, it was obvious by the peeling paint and
crumbling steps, that proper upkeep had not been a
priority.

Parker used the tarnished brass doorknocker to
announce his presence. He was greeted at the door by
a housekeeper. "May I help you?"

"Yes! I am looking for Dr. Thomas Armstrong."

"Dr. Armstrong is out of town on business, and we don't know when to expect him. I am Renee, the housekeeper. Is there something I can help you with?"

Flashing his badge, "I am Agent Richard Parker with the SB. I have some questions for him regarding a case I am working on."

"He has been unreachable for the past few days," she said, a fact Parker was already well aware of.

Taking a business card from his pocket, he presented it to her. "Please have him get in touch with me as soon as possible. It is extremely urgent. I have some questions for him regarding a homicide."

"Oh, dear!" She accepted the card and looked down at it. "I will make sure he gets this message as soon as I hear from him!"

The woman closed the door and as he turned, he noticed some movement from a curtain on the second floor. Though the face was concealed, he could make out the outline of a woman. He stopped and watched her until she moved away.

"It's strange she never leaves the house, isn't it?" muttered the postman making his rounds as he stuffed the mail in the receptacle.

"I beg your pardon?"

"Mrs. Armstrong! They say she is addled in the mind and that Dr. Armstrong keeps her confined for her own safety."

Parker's face clouded over. "Did you say, *Mrs.* Armstrong?"

"Yes!"

"Would that be his mother?" Parker was now standing in front of the man, appearing confused.

"No, that would be his wife."

"Dr. Armstrong is married?"

The carrier nodded, stopping to look up at the window. "Yes, he is. I have been on this route for ten years and I have never seen her outside. It's rather sad." Sifting through the mail in his hands, he continued on his way. "Have a good day!"

"Yes, and you as well!" Parker stood dumbstruck. Stroking his chin, he tried to figure out how best to handle the situation. The fact occurred to him that with Thomas out of the picture, it was of little matter that he had a wife. The danger was gone and the less the 'lady of the house' knew, the better, especially if she were as delicate as the man said. In truth, she was just as well off without him, whether she knew it or not. On the other hand, it was a loose end, and the woman would eventually deserve to have some closure. He could just walk away and forget the whole thing, but— damn him! That man was in the wind, literally, and still wreaking havoc on the world.

Parker returned to his car and sat in the driver's seat for a bit before taking out his phone. Curiosity and conscience getting the better of him, he dialed up Benji Phelps, his right-hand man and expert researcher at the SB. If there was a stone to be overturned, he was the man to find it. He answered on the first ring.

"Hey boss, what's up?"

"Benji! I need you to do a search for a marriage license for our dear Dr. Armstrong. I was just informed he has a wife."

Leaning with his feet propped on the desk studying a codex, Benji tossed it aside. "You know, I am a little insulted. There is no possible way I would have missed something as simple as that."

"I know! I know! You're the best and all that jazz! Just check again anyway!" Parker ordered.

"Does it really matter if he's gone?" Benji grumbled, righting himself in front of his twelve computer screens.

"Not really, I suppose, but if he does, we will have to eventually provide some sort of answer for her sake."

"I don't see why," he muttered as he tapped on his keyboard. "I am telling you, that man does—rather did—NOT have a wife. I would have known about it. From what we have learned of that bastard, she's probably just someone he brought home for the night, and she never left."

"He doesn't strike me as the type."

"Well, he must be! I just ran it again across the board and there is no marriage record for Thomas Armstrong anywhere."

Parker looked towards the house. "Huh!"

"Unless he is one of those extra sick puppies who shags his sister," Benji added with disgust, "which would be impossible because he was an only child." He rocked his chair back. "He was the last member of his family, and he is dead. Forget about it! We have plenty of the living to be concerned with. And, while you are sitting in London brooding over nothing, there is a lovely young archaeologist waiting for you in

North Elmham. Why don't you get back to her and enjoy a few days in her bed before the next antichrist starts to rear his ugly head?"

"You're probably right! I am going to take some time off and I will see you in a couple of weeks." Parker started the car and paused. "But keep an eye out just the same. I don't want something coming out of nowhere to bite us in the ass."

"Will do, boss!" acknowledged Benji before shutting off the phone and reaching for his puzzle box.

Renee pressed her back to the door and growled. If the SB was nosing around, it must have meant things had gone badly in North Elmham. She had been unable to reach Thomas, which meant he was probably dead. It might be for the best anyway. The man was a little too ambitious and absorbed in his own agenda. At least he had served his purpose before he departed. The child that had been conceived during the ceremony was now in the world, and her father was no longer necessary. Things would go more smoothly without him.

"Who was that?" called Bethany from the top of the stairs, cradling Millie in her arms.

"A pesky salesman," she lied, tossing the card into the trash bin. "But I have good news. While you were napping, Dr. Armstrong called."

"Why didn't you wake me?"

"Because you are a nursing mother, and you need your rest."

"Well, what did he say?"

Renee started up the stairs. "He is thrilled beyond measure about the baby's arrival and cannot wait to meet her. It seems he got bogged down in problems at the worksite and will not have time to return home before moving to the next job. Instead, he wants us to close up here and move to the Manchester house where he will join us as soon as he can."

"The Manchester house? What Manchester house and why?"

"The Armstrong family has homes all over. I am sure Thomas has mentioned it. He is beginning a new job there, and he will be much closer." Renee stopped to take the baby. "I am going to put her down for a nap and start packing."

"But I don't want to leave here," Bethany protested. "This is our home."

"Suit yourself, but I do work for Dr. Armstrong, and he wants his daughter in Manchester. I have my orders. Then again, I can always take the baby without you."

"NO! My baby remains with me, no matter what! I don't care what anyone says!"

"Good! Then it is settled." Renee smiled and started towards the nursery, a tinge of black flashing in her eyes as she walked away. "I will have your things ready to go by morning." Stopping in the doorway, she called over her shoulder, "Did you forget to take your pills today? You know how upset you become without them."

"No, I took them," Bethany replied. "And I will pack my own things."

Once Renee was gone, Bethany descended the staircase, glancing over her shoulder as she fished the card from the trash. "SB? What the heck is the SB?" she asked herself. When she heard Renee moving around, she quickly stuffed it in her pocket and moved out of sight.

He came home with flowers and wine in hand to find Cassie lying in bed reading.

"I was beginning to think I had scared you off," she said, closing her book and tossing it aside. "You aren't afraid of witches, are you?"

"Not in the least," he said, leaning down to kiss her. "Some of my favorite people are witches."

"Those for me or do you have another hot date with someone else?"

"I only have eyes for you, sweetheart" he replied with a weary sigh.

Cassie could tell something was bothering him. "Want to talk about it?"

"Not really," he set the items aside and sat down on the edge of the bed, taking her hand in his. "Right now, I just want to lock myself in this room with you for the next two weeks and spend the rest of my life getting lost in your eyes."

Pulling him to her by his tie, she grinned. "Well, we had better get started. The rest of our lives might not be long enough, and we have quite a bit of catching up to do."

11

CHAPTER ELEVEN

The following Spring

London

Adam Belek sighed heavily. Some days his job sucked, and this day was no different. When he became a private investigator, he had grand illusions of becoming a real-life Sherlock Holmes, solving crimes, earning prestige, and making the world a safer place. Instead, he found himself being the bearer of bad news, the finder of lost dogs, and the ruin of many a marriage. Today would be no different. He rang the doorbell and was immediately met by an anxious young American woman.

"Come in!" She hurried him inside and looked around nervously before closing the door. "In there, please. We don't have much time before the housekeeper returns. I don't want her to know that I hired you." She pointed towards a sofa. "Now, will you please tell me what you found out?"

"Of course!" He took a seat and opened his satchel. "I am sorry to be the one to tell you this, Mrs. Armstrong, but I think you need to accept the fact your husband is not coming home," he explained. "It has been six months and not a soul has seen him."

Bethany ran her hand over the edge of the bassinet where Millie was napping, watching through the window for Renee's return. She had sent her out on errands, not wanting the housekeeper to know what she was up to. "I don't accept that! He wanted this child more than anything. Why would he leave me after giving him something he wanted so badly? Something else must have happened to him."

She remembered the night Millie had been conceived. He was sweet and attentive, taking her to a fancy inn in the middle of nowhere for the weekend. He had rented out the whole place, so they were completely alone. They drank wine—so much wine, in fact, that wonderful night had turned into a bit of a magical haze. It was like a faraway dream, bits and pieces of reality mixed with wonderments that could not possibly be. The thick, sweet drink had been so potent that, at one point, she had imagined others in the room with them, though he reassured her with laughs and kisses, it was all in her head. On their return home, she felt refreshed, rejuvenated, and loved.

It had been years since they connected and had seemingly grown apart. Most days she felt like a burden to him, a responsibility placed on him many years before. A terrible accident had robbed her of her memories. Thomas had filled in the details, explaining how she was in her last year of college and that they had been dating when it happened. He had planned an impromptu weekend hike for them, and halfway through, she had slipped on the rocks, falling to a ledge below, banging her head. She woke up in the hospital with Thomas by her side, holding her hand, telling her how much he loved her and how he was going to take good care of her. Not a sliver of a memory from before that day had ever returned. It was all a complete blank.

When she had questioned why no family had ever visited, he explained she had none left, both her parents having died before she ever started college. A few days after the accident, he had her medically moved to his home in London where she had been ever since. He hired a nurse to ensure she remembered to take her meds and look after her and made sure Renee, the housekeeper, was always there for whatever she needed. He had begun to go away on business for more extended periods of time, and she had seen less and less of him over the years. Bethany expected him to come home any day and ask for a divorce, but instead, that weekend, he came home with roses and wine, profusely apologizing for not being there more often for her and for neglecting her feelings. He said he loved her and wanted more than anything to start over by beginning a family together. She had never remembered being happier.

"Perhaps the thought of fatherhood was too much for him, or maybe he fell in love with someone else. I can't say for sure, but what I do know, is that he is not here because he doesn't want to be. You might want to look at this." He handed her the paperwork he didn't want to show to her, especially being a new mother, but she did pay him for the truth. "His credit cards were used in London a week after you gave birth. It is obvious he has gone into hiding."

"What? No! That doesn't make any sense!" she snatched it from his hand. "Thomas would never—there must be some sort of mistake. Besides, he sent for us, telling us to come here. Why would he do that and not show up?"

"The contractor he was working for was murdered. An arrest warrant was issued for your husband shortly after. The authorities believe he wanted Thomas to halt all work, but Thomas wanted to continue digging and a confrontation ensued."

"And you think that is a motive for murder? What kind of sense does that make?" Bethany shook her head. "Where was he last seen?"

The man took a report from his briefcase and handed it to her. "On the job in North Elmham. The family does have that little place on the water out there. His truck is parked there, but I staked it out for several days, and he never showed up. In fact, by the looks of things, the vehicle hasn't moved in months. He was working with another archaeologist, but I have been unable to catch up with her. It seems she travels quite a bit."

"She?"

He nodded. "An archaeologist by the name of Cassie Summers. I have her information. Would you like me to continue trying to reach her?"

"Cassie Summers? I have never heard him mention that name." Bethany shook her head and looked down at the baby. "No, I will go myself. It's time I got some answers about what my husband has been up to."

After the man left, she went to a safe and removed several stacks of cash. Thomas had never given her access to any kind of money for herself, but she had happened upon the combination numbers in a desk drawer while looking for something else. She had been astonished at the amount but was grateful to have it at her disposal. Rushing upstairs, she quickly threw together a suitcase for her and one for the baby, calling for a taxi on the way to the door. If she calculated right, she might make it to the train station before Renee knew she was gone. Something was terribly wrong, and she needed to find Thomas to get some answers.

North Elmham

"I still can't believe you convinced that contractor's family to donate the land," said Cassie as she and Parker strolled hand in hand through the gardens that had been opened to the public that day.

"The funny thing was—nobody seemed to want it. Something about it being cursed, although I can't imagine why!" He grinned and kissed the top of her head.

"It's beautiful and I cannot think of a more fitting way to honor our sisters," remarked Sadie, taking Jessie by the hand and leaning against her. "They would have loved it!"

The Haven was the town's newest addition, a small botanical garden with an entire area dedicated to heirloom herbs, as well as being the only place in the world silphium grew, thanks to the discovery of the seeds in Sadie's pocket upon their return. In the center of the grounds were thirteen flat stones, in a circle marking the graves of each coven member who gave her life to protect the others. Their names were inscribed, honoring them as early citizens of the town, but also with discreet symbols only recognizable by those who practiced the arts. In the center where Selena had been imprisoned all those years was a fountain with an opal witch's globe in the center that sparkled when the sun shone down.

After Selena was contained, the globe was taken back to the salt cave, where it was placed in a safe place. Formal charges of murder and a warrant were issued for Thomas's arrest so it would appear he just ran off.

Cassie had joined up with Parker in more ways than one. Not only had she become part of the special branch of the SB as its resident archaeologist, but the two had just purchased a house together not far from The Witch's Globe. They spent their time hunting down artifacts and those who sought to use them for nefarious purposes. In addition to that, she was always searching the records for extended family members. They had located nine, all with gifts of their own, who they found were interested in learning more. Sadie had turned out to be a wonderful instructor and was happy to share her knowledge when she and Jessie weren't busy cooking for the guests of the inn, which had become quite a popular destination, drawing in those interested in the occult.

The coven was growing once more and Cassie was exceeding expectations as its new leader, her abilities growing by leaps and bounds each day after accepting the reality of who she was.

In addition, just the week before, a ribbon-cutting had been held for the newly built historical museum, dedicated to Ilene's memory. They all attended knowing how honored Ilene would have been by the gesture.

"Would you care to join me under the rowan tree by the koi pond?" Parker asked Cassie.

"I would be delighted," she replied, taking his arm. "You two coming?"

"No! I think we are going…over here," Jessie pointed to the herb garden, knowing full well Parker intended to propose that afternoon. "Enjoy yourselves!" she said with a slight grin on her face before she and Sadie scampered off giggling.

"What was that all about?"

"No idea!" he lied, a sly smirk on his lips as he patted his jacket pocket for the hundredth time that day. Locating an empty bench beneath the tree, he helped her to sit and took the seat next to her.

"Is everything okay?" she teased.

In truth, she had gotten a read on him when she kissed him the day he came home with the ring nearly a month ago, her ability to tap into the flow of life around her having grown exponentially. Her vision that day showed her he had spent nearly three hours looking at every diamond in the store until he found just the right one—and it was perfect.

He leaned back, crossed his legs, and rested his arm on the back of the bench. "Everything is wonderful and has been since the day you came into my life!"

"Cassie, there is so much I want to say to you," he grinned, "but you already know how I feel. Just like I know you know what I am up to now."

A smile crossed her lips, and she lifted her chin, pressing her lips together. "I don't know what you mean," she said, pretending to be affronted.

"I never believed in 'love at first sight', 'true love', or 'soulmates', but then I met you. There isn't any way possible I can vocalize how much I love you, but the great thing about us is that we don't need to speak the words."

"Oh, I think I would like to hear the words," she whispered. "A girl only gets proposed to by her soulmate once in a lifetime."

"Fair enough!" He couldn't contain the joy on his face. "I love you more than anything in this world, Cassie Summers, and I would be honored if you would say 'yes'." He dropped to one knee and pulled the ring box from his pocket. "Will you marry me?"

"Yes, Agent Richard Parker, I would love to marry you!"

She wrapped her arms around his neck and enthusiastically kissed him.

"Did I get the right ring?" he asked.

"You have to open the box first," she replied.

"Like you haven't already seen it," he said with a whimsical roll of an eye, lifting the lid.

"I do appreciate the fact you went through the whole store!"

He slipped it on her finger.

"It's perfect and I cannot wait to spend the rest of my life with you!"

Jessie and Sadie were watching from behind a nearby tree.

"You can come out now!"

They rushed over and embraced the happy couple. It was a wonderful day and just the beginning of their new life together.

Epilogue

Bethany held the baby carrier on her arm as she stepped off the train. This was the last place Thomas was seen and a good place to start. She would have answers for her and her daughter, no matter what.

Seeing a porter on the platform, she waved him over and pressed several rolled-up bills into his palm. "Can you help me please? I am new here. I need help with my luggage, and a recommendation for a good place to stay." The older gentleman looked down at the wad of cash and smiled.

"Certainly ma'am!" he answered in a heavy Scottish accent. "Don't ye worry about a thing. Just hand me yer luggage ticket and I will take care of it straight away. I noticed an Uber without a passenger in the parking lot. Why don't I grab him and have ye taken to the best inn in town?"

"And where would that be?"

"A lovely little place called 'The Witch's Globe'. I have a feeling ye won't be disappointed."

"Thank you, but I will also be requiring something else."

"What's that, ma'am?"

"Your discretion. If anyone asks, I was never here."

"Of course! Whatever you say!"

The man escorted her to the waiting car and loaded her bags into the trunk as she got herself and the baby settled inside. Just before closing the top, he discreetly slid the wad of cash she had slipped to him into the top of the baby's diaper bag and removed several pill bottles from the side of her carry-on. "This certainly is some nasty stuff," he muttered as he slipped them into his pocket.

"Yer all set!" he called out as he banged on the side of the car. "I hope ye and the bairn enjoy yer stay, lass! Take care of yerself!"

"Thank you so much for your help!" she waved to him as they pulled away.

Finn waited for them to be out of sight before removing his cap and dropping it, and the pill bottles, into a nearby trash can. Brushing his hands together, he sighed. The two paths were now set to cross and there was nothing to do but wait and see what would happen next. "It will be interesting to see how this all shakes out, especially without those pesky pills that have been clouding her mind all these years!" he muttered as he walked away from the station, his form slowly dissipating into a trail of golden light as he went.

About the Author

Tempie W. Wade is the award-winning author of The Timely Revolution Book Series, a Revolutionary War time-travel adventure.

Her first book, A Timely Revolution, was awarded best historical fantasy in the 2019 American Book Fest American Fiction Awards.

The writer is a lifelong resident of Virginia and currently resides in Williamsburg.

For more information, please visit,
www.TempieWade.com

The Timely Revolution Book Series is a work of historical fiction/fantasy based during the Revolutionary War with the added element of Celtic Fae lore. The first book, A Timely Revolution, won Best Historical Fantasy in the American Book Fest American Fiction Awards for 2019. Books are available on Amazon.

The Timely Revolution Book Series in Order:

Book One-A Timely Revolution

Book Two-More

Book Three- The Complicated Life of Maggie MacGregor

Book Four-Timely Revelations

Book Five- The Steep Cost of Fate

Book Six-Secrets and Lies

Book Seven-Children of the Gods

Book Eight-TBA

Book Nine-TBA

Book Ten-TBA

☐

A Spy Among Them
by Tempie W. Wade

All is fair in love and war when a devilishly handsome rogue holds the key to what you desire most! Young Emma Eldridge is introduced to the harsh existence of living under British rule when she becomes the sole witness to the murders of her beloved parents at the hand of one of their leaders. With no other living relatives left in the world, she is taken in by her 'spinster' aunt, Lucile Wolfe of New York, who is anything but an innocent little old lady.

Thirteen years later, in the year 1779, America is in the midst of a brutal battle for independence from England, and New York is currently controlled by the British army. Emma and her Aunt Lucy are now not only the most desired socialites in town but the biggest source of information for the opposing army regarding troop movements within the city. Their normally easy endeavors become a bit more complicated with the arrival of the keen and charismatic Major John André, the newly appointed British Head of Intelligence. Emma must redouble her efforts to protect the secrets they keep while continuing to further the Patriot cause. Her focus shifts dramatically, however, when she discovers Major André in the possession of a letter signed by a man she vowed to kill, and she will risk anything to exact her revenge — even if it costs her everything.

www.TempieWade.com